D1125557

The Billionaire's Beck & Call:
The Complete Series

Delilah Fawkes

DEDICATION

To my husband, who always punishes me when I'm naughty as well as when I'm very, very good.

CONTENTS

1   At His Service   Pg 3

2   At His Mercy   Pg 17

3   At His Command   Pg 34

4   At His Insistence   Pg 48

5   At His Instruction   Pg 67

6   At His Word   Pg 85

7   At His Desire   Pg 105

8   At His Warning   Pg 124

9   At His Side   Pg 140

10   Bonus Story: My Best Friend's Brother   Pg 157

ACKNOWLEDGMENTS

To all my dear friends on EWS, my goons over on Something Awful as well as those who first got me started over on the Kindle Boards. Thank you for all of your help, wisdom and inspiration! You've helped make it possible for me to work my dream job, and I've never been happier. May all of your wildest dreams come true, especially if they involve spankings!

1 AT HIS SERVICE

I pushed my glasses up the bridge of my nose and sighed as I stared at the papers I'd dropped. This was shaping up to be the worst day ever, and it was only my second day on the job. First, I'd lost a contact and had to break out my clunky emergency glasses, then the CEO's assistant called in sick before the biggest stockholder meeting of the year.

Of course, they'd called me in to assist, even though she was only the front desk receptionist.

If all Mr. Drake wants me to do is answer phones, I've got this in the bag. I rolled my eyes, knowing it couldn't possibly be that easy.

I hadn't met Chase Drake yet, billionaire CEO of Drake & Smith, but I'd heard whispered rumors about him over lunch. Words like "terrifying" and "gorgeous" were thrown around, along with talk of all the other executive assistants that quit unexpectedly that year. Apparently, he was impossible to please.

I dropped to my knees, hurriedly gathering the papers outside of the executive offices. *This is no way to make a first impression, Isabeau! Get it together or you won't last the week.* The last thing I needed was for the head honcho to see me like this.

A black, Italian leather shoe came down an inch from my

hand. I froze, still reaching for the spreadsheet now trapped under the large foot in front of me. It was attached to a leg clad in an impeccably cut suit, and as I ran my eyes upward, I tried not to tremble. A man with wavy blonde hair and a cool green gaze stared down at me, his cruel mouth twisted into a smirk.

"Ms. Willcox, I presume?"

I tried to push the chestnut strands of hair that had fallen over my eyes back into my bun, but it was no good. I was a hot mess, kneeling on the carpet in a J.C. Penney blouse and skirt.

"Y-yes?"

He reached down and offered his hand, and my mouth suddenly went very, *very* dry. I'm talking Sahara Desert dry. Something about the way he looked at me sent shivers down my spine, like he was sizing me up. Like I was a deer, and he was a lion, looking for his next meal.

I put my hand in his, and let him pull me to my feet. My hand felt tiny in his warm grasp, and I felt a jolt of electricity at the touch.

"Chase Drake," he said softly, his low voice making my heart skip a beat. "So, you're the one serving me today?"

Serving him? It felt like an odd way to put it, but hey, who was I to correct the boss?

"I guess so, Sir."

"You guess?"

I realized my hand was still in his, and quickly drew it back. "Ms. Johnson told me you needed an assistant for the meeting?"

I bit my lip, suddenly uncertain. His piercing eyes were hard to look directly into. I felt like I was being tested, or maybe that I was in the wrong place altogether.

"Keep your chin up, girl. My assistant must be cool, confident and collected, not a timid little mouse."

My mouth dropped open. A mouse? He doesn't even know me! I raised my chin defiantly, straightening up to my full height.

"Yes, Sir."

His lips twitched into a half smile. "Very good."

I nodded, and started walking toward the boardroom, when he grabbed my wrist, making me gasp. He drew me close until we were almost nose to nose.

"Remember that you represent *me* in there. Clean yourself up before we begin. And Ms. Willcox?"

"Y-yes?"

"Don't let me down."

I tried hard not to tremble, even though he'd pulled me so close. He smelled clean like rainwater, but his hot breath on my face made me avert my eyes. Is this how he always acted? So demanding and confrontational?

"Will do, Boss."

I snatched my wrist away and moved quickly down the hall to the ladies room. I could feel his gaze on my back until the door closed behind me. When it clicked shut, I leaned back against it, and let out a deep breath.

What an asshole.

I was beginning to wonder if the executive assistant was really sick, or if she was just sick of his domineering bullshit. But, despite my irritation, my wrist tingled where he'd held me, and I couldn't stop thinking about those eyes of his, that strong jaw... and how I wanted to run my hands through that gorgeous wavy hair of his.

"Get over it, Isa. Never gonna happen," I muttered to myself.

Whoa. Where did that *come from?*

I mean, sure, he was amazing looking, and from the moment his eyes met mine, I felt a magnetism radiating off him, drawing me to him, but that didn't mean I was interested. Far from it, after the way he'd just spoken to me.

I ran my hands under the sink and slicked my hair back, redoing my bun as best I could at the nape of my neck. My hair was always unruly and wild. I just hoped it would stay put for the next hour. I retouched my light makeup, and looked at myself in the mirror.

It would have to do.

I took a deep breath, and readied myself to face Mr. Drake.

***

The meeting went off without a hitch. I sat next to the CEO running his slides as he presented to the table full of crusty old men. Standing before them, speaking so smoothly and confidently, the juxtaposition of his youth and power against the rest of them was not lost on me. He moved with the kind of grace and power you'd expect of royalty, commanding the attention and respect of everyone in the room.

At the end, as the board members filed out into the hallway, he came up behind me and put a hand on my shoulder. I flinched beneath his touch.

"Meet me in my office in half an hour."

I pursed my lips, a spike of fear coursing through me. Had I done something wrong? Was I getting fired? It would officially be the shortest temp job ever. What would my friends say when they heard I'd gotten canned on my second day?

"Yes, Sir," I squeaked.

He swept out of the room, and I heard him laughing and joking with the other men as they moved down the hall. I put my head down and packed up his notes and laptop, trying to get my shit together as I worked.

Calm down, Isa. What will be, will be.

I pictured those cool eyes staring at me as he mouthed the words "We're letting you go," and felt a shiver creep down my spine. For some reason, the look of disappointment I pictured on his handsome face was the worst part.

***

I rapped on the mahogany door at the end of the executive wing, and tried to steady my breathing.

"Come in."

"Here goes nothing," I whispered, and entered the office, trying to hold my chin high.

Mr. Drake looked up at me, his green eyes intense, but the emotion behind them unreadable. Was he angry with me? Had I embarrassed him somehow? I was so inexperienced, I was positive it wasn't good.

"Ms. Willcox, come here."

I smoothed my hands over my skirt and took a few steps toward the chairs in front of his desk.

"Did I say you could sit there? Come here. To me."

I paused, shifting uncomfortably on my feet.

"Are you deaf? I said come *here*."

His sharp tone sent a shiver down my spine. I set my jaw and walked around the desk until I was just inches away from him. He spun in his chair toward me slowly and leaned back, a smirk playing over his handsome face. For a long moment, he just looked me over, appraising me, then staring into my eyes to see if I would look away, I suppose.

I didn't.

"Take a seat here. On the desk."

His voice was a low whisper, his eyes intense.

I hesitated the briefest of moments, but then a little voice inside my head said *He's messing with you. He wants to see if you're afraid.* I glared back at him. I needed to show him he didn't intimidate me, no matter how rich and powerful he was.

I hopped up on the edge of his desk, and crossed my bare legs demurely. His eyes roamed over my exposed skin, stopping at my hem line, before moving up my body to my breasts, straining beneath my blouse. I tried to keep my breathing steady, but I felt so vulnerable this close to him, especially when he looked at me like that.

"What do you know about me, Isabeau?"

He leaned forward, and I forced myself to stay still

instead of shying away. He was so close that I could smell the subtle notes of his cologne: musk and wood with a hint of leather.

"My apologies… May I call you Isabeau?" He smiled up at me, dazzling me for a moment.

"Of course." My voice sounded high and breathy. I gripped the edge of his desk, trying not to fidget.

"Good. What have you heard about me, Isabeau? What do you really know about me?"

What did he want me to say? That everyone said he was an ogre? Or that they all wanted to sleep with him anyway?

"I…"

"Go on. You won't hurt my feelings."

He was still smiling, slight dimples visible in both cheeks. The sight was distracting, to say the least.

"I know that you're the youngest CEO and partner in the company's history, and I know that you earned the spot by working your way up after graduate school instead of using your inheritance as a crutch."

"Everyone knows that. What do you *know* about me? The real stuff. None of this press release bullshit."

I looked down at my hands, anything not to have to look up at his face so close to me.

"Um. People say… they say that you're scary. And that your assistants don't last long."

He laughed, a deep, warm sound that seemed to fill up the office. I glanced up to see him smirking at me. I relaxed my grip on the desk a little. Maybe I wasn't being fired after all.

"What else do they say?"

Oh, God. He can't possibly want me to tell him everything. Does he? The look on his face confirmed that he did. It was clear by the way he looked at me that I wasn't leaving this office until I gave him exactly what he wanted.

"They say. Um… They say that you're very, uh, good looking… and impossible to please."

"Oh they do, do they?" He sat back, and tented his

fingers beneath his chin. "Well, do you agree with them? Do you think I'm scary, handsome and woefully unsatisfied?"

My mouth dropped open, and I quickly closed it with a snap.

"Yes. I mean, *no!* I mean, I don't know…"

He stood, then, and leaned in close, towering over me. "You were right the first time."

Anxiety coursed through me, but I have to admit, being this close to him, smelling his scent and feeling the heat radiating off his body, it made me wonder what it would be like to be in his arms. To be his. To be owned by him…

His face was almost touching mine when he whispered to me. "I *am* unsatisfied, Isabeau. I want you to be my new assistant. Will you do that for me? Will you be at my beck and call?"

My breath left me as his words sunk in. When I finally regained it, I felt like I was trembling from head to toe. *His beck and call.*

"Wh-what about your old assistant?"

Mr. Drake leaned back again and took my chin in his hand, forcing my eyes to his. "What about her? I want *you.*"

His touch on my skin was electric. *Are we still talking about business?*

"Yes, Mr. Drake."

His thumb stroked my cheek for the briefest of moments, and then he released me, breathless, and wondering what I'd just agreed to.

"Very good, Isabeau. I'll expect you here at 8 a.m. tomorrow, in my office, ready to work. Don't be late."

He turned away, effectively dismissing me. I hopped down off the desk and quickly made for the door. I didn't want to give him time to change his mind.

"And Isabeau?"

I turned back, my hand on the knob. "Yes, Mr. Drake?"

"I don't tolerate sloppy work. Disappoint me, and there will be consequences."

I blushed, and nodded, then closed the door behind me.

What had I gotten myself into?

***

"Isabeau! Get in here, now!"

I jumped in my seat in front of the big, mahogany doors, spilling my cup of ramen noodles onto my blouse.

"Shit! Shit, shit, *shit*." If there was one thing Mr. Drake hated, it was sloppiness, and here I was dripping with cheap soup stock. My silk was stained, the material sticking to the tops of my breasts.

"By now, I meant immediately, Isabeau! Not at your personal convenience."

I swore again under my breath, and entered his office. Maybe a miracle would occur, and he wouldn't notice. Please, God, have mercy!

"Sit," he commanded.

I moved toward the chairs once again, but he stared at me, frowning, until I circled the desk and perched on the edge.

"Yes, Mr. Drake?"

"What took you so long? I need you to type these notes up for me, and…"

He stopped, sniffing the air. He leaned in, and to my horror, plucked a long, wavy noodle out of my cleavage. I bit my lip, tears of embarrassment burning behind my eyes.

I had to keep it together. It probably wasn't the end of the world, even though it felt like it, sitting here in front of my boss, who could have been a GQ model, shaking with nerves, and dripping with soup.

"Oh, my dear," he said, placing it into his trashcan like it was a dead spider. "This is not good at all. I don't like this. One. Little. *Bit.*"

He was out of his chair in a flash, and before I could stop him, his hands were on my blouse, undoing my buttons with speed and precision.

"Mr. Drake!"

He ripped the last button off, and I winced as the silk tore. My shirt fell open, revealing my bra, and he yanked it down off my shoulders and threw it to the floor.

"I thought I made it clear that I do not tolerate sloppiness?"

His voice was deep and dripping with menace. I tried to cover myself, but he slapped my hands away and ran his eyes over my exposed curves without a hint of embarrassment.

"You represent me, Isabeau. *Me!* And I do not present myself in such a disgusting manner. Not to my colleagues. Not to anyone."

He leaned forward, caging me in with a hand on each side of my body. His face was just an inch from mine, his clean breath tickling my lips. What was he going to do to me?

"I… I'm sorry," I breathed.

"Sorry's not going to cut it, girl. You seem to have a problem remembering what my rules are. You've been lax. Lazy. Disheveled. I think it's high time you were punished."

He toyed with one of my bra straps, then slid it slowly down one shoulder. I tensed, wondering how far he would go. Fear coursed through me, but at the same time, my heart raced, my sex heating against the surface of the desk. I had to admit it, even if it was just to myself…

I wanted him.

There was something mesmerizing about him. Something forceful and dangerous. Something I couldn't resist, even if I wanted to. And I wasn't sure that I did.

"You need to remember who you belong to." His voice was a low growl now as he traced the top of my breasts with a long finger.

Was this really happening? I suppressed a moan, suppressed the desire to reach up and run my hands through his hair, to pull his mouth down to mine.

"You need a punishment you won't soon forget."

He backed away, and I felt his absence like a tangible thing.

"Turn around and place your hands flat on the desk."

I gasped, looking at him in disbelief. Had I heard him right? Part of me wondered if he was going to raise my skirt, jerk my panties down around my ankles, and fuck me right then and there. And if he did, would I let him? Would I stay bent over while my billionaire boss used me for his pleasure?

My pussy heated at the thought. A man like him wanting me was almost too much to handle.

I did as I was told and placed my palms flat on the desk, leaning over as I did so. I waited for him to grip my zipper; to rip my skirt off my body or push it up over my hips. I was ready to be his. To be possessed.

His hand came down hard on my ass, making me yell in surprise. I winced, my eyes watering from the impact. I wanted to look at Mr. Drake, to ask what he was thinking, but something kept my hands firmly on the desk, helpless beneath him.

"You've been very bad," he growled.

His hand came down again with a *smack* that took my breath away. I mewled as the stinging washed over me, but held my place, not wanting to disappoint him.

Despite the pain, my panties were wet, my pussy ready for him. I felt helpless and sensual and wild, like never before. Who was this Isabeau bending over for her boss? I didn't know her, but I also didn't want to stop feeling this way.

"You will not disobey me!"

Another blow made me yelp, then another, reddening the same spots he'd hit before, making my ass burn beneath the thin material of my skirt. I felt the bruises forming, and bit my lip, trying not to scream as his hand came down again and again. The office echoed with the sound of his hand cracking down mercilessly on my tender flesh, and my panting as I stood there and took every blow, legs shaking, pussy glowing with need for this man.

Finally, he paused, and I felt him lift the hem of my skirt up and over my ass. I whimpered as the fabric grazed my abused skin.

"Let's see if you've learned your lesson…"

I knew he must be admiring his handiwork, leaning over me, inspecting my backside, on display for him.

"Oh yes. This punishment should be a constant reminder over the next few days to behave. Every time you sit, you'll remember this little lesson."

His hand smoothed over my ass, clad only in my sheer, white panties. I gasped as he squeezed the bruised flesh, and felt my face burning with shame. I knew he could see the wet spot between my legs. What must he think of me?

"What is this, Isabeau?" His voice was a dangerous rumble. "I can smell your arousal from here. My nostrils are filled with it..."

His hands kneaded my ass cheeks roughly, making me moan in pain.

"Look at you. Look at this!"

His fingers forced their way past the thin cotton mesh of my underwear and dipped roughly into my wetness. I squirmed against his touch, and his hand came down on my ass again, making me burn all over.

"You little slut. You're loving this, aren't you?"

He spanked me again and again, all the while pumping two fingers into my tight, eager channel. I was yelling then, my body squeezing around him with each stroke. I couldn't believe he was doing this, and what was more, I was enjoying every second. Just like he said.

"Answer me when I speak to you, Isabeau!"

Mr. Drake's fingers increased speed, making me moan loudly into the desk.

"Are you enjoying this? Do you think this is a game?"

He spanked me harder, slamming my hips into the wood as he finger fucked me. I was so close to cumming, but I tried to hold it back. I didn't know what his reaction would be if I came undone beneath him.

"Yes!" I breathed. "I mean, no. It's... ahhhh... it's not a game..."

"You're goddamn right, it's not a game!"

Mr. Drake reached around my body and pinched my clit

viciously. And just like that, I was cumming, wailing as my pussy convulsed around his fingers, waves of pleasure and pain making me soar to heights I didn't know I was capable of. He went still inside of me, his fingers filling me as I squeezed tight with each pulse, flying on wings of ecstasy.

When I finally came back down to Earth, he pulled his fingers out of me and jerked my skirt back down. I turned around, breathing hard, in time to see him wiping his hand on his silk pocket square, avoiding my eyes.

He opened his bottom desk drawer and threw a white dress shirt at me. One of his spares.

"Get out."

I caught it, my brow furrowing. "Mr. Drake?"

"I said, *get out.*"

The dangerous tone in his voice left no room for discussion. I pulled the shirt around my shoulders and hurried out, buttoning as I went.

Back at my desk, I tried to fight back the tears, without success. What the hell had just happened? Did he want me or not? Had I disappointed him somehow? Just when my fantasies were coming true... I wasn't good enough.

***

At the end of the night, as Mr. Drake left his office, he paused beside me. I remained looking forward, responding to an email, not daring to speak. What would I say if I did? A warm hand on my shoulder made me jump.

"Isabeau, I..."

I looked up and was caught up again in those cool, green eyes. For a moment, I thought I caught a hint of sadness behind them, but then it faded, his unreadable mask slipping back into place.

"Yes, Mr. Drake?"

"What happened today... It was wrong of me. For a moment, I forgot myself. You make me do that, you know."

He paused, looking me over, taking in his oversized shirt

falling low over my pencil skirt.

"Do what?" I asked, allowing myself a small smile.

"Forget myself."

He leaned down, and I heard him inhale, millimeters away. Was he smelling my hair? Then, he straightened again, his back stiff. Formal. Like nothing had passed between us.

"It won't happen again. It... *can't.* I won't lose my temper again. Not with you."

He moved away, and I jumped out of my seat, following like a lost puppy.

"But, why not? I don't mind!"

He stopped by the elevators, hesitating before pushing the button.

"I... I liked it," I said, my voice barely a whisper.

A moment hung suspended before he finally moved, pushing the down button with a black, gloved hand.

"I won't punish you again, Isabeau. Not like that. This was the first and last time. Please understand."

The doors slid open, and just like that, he was gone, sliding away from me into the night. And I could do nothing to stop him.

I looked down at the ramen cup sticking out of my trashcan, and a thought struck me, lifting the cloud of confusion and despair threatening to settle over me. Maybe there was a way.

Maybe I was a very bad, lazy, forgetful assistant after all. Maybe I just couldn't help myself. Maybe I'd just have to break his rules...

Maybe then he wouldn't be able to help it, and would forget himself all over again.

I bit my lip and leaned back in the office chair, imaging him bending me over his desk, guiding his cock toward my eager sex. I slipped a finger beneath my skirt, rubbing myself through my panties, wondering what it would feel like to have him inside of me. My ass stung as I pressed back onto my wooden chair, and I moaned, remembering his sweet punishment.

I knew one thing for certain--this wasn't over between us. Not by a long shot.

I was his, after all, at his beck and call. Ready and eager for whatever he had to give me.

2 AT HIS MERCY

"Isabeau! Get in here this instant!"

A shiver of anticipation raced down my spine and I allowed myself time for a smile before jumping up from my desk. This was the second time Mr. Drake called me into his office today, and from his tone, he sounded like he was about to lose it. Just as I'd planned.

I eased open the mahogany door and slipped inside, checking my hair to make sure it hadn't escaped its chignon. Mr. Drake sat on the edge of his desk facing the doorway, perched like a bird of prey. His wavy hair was perfectly in place, but his green eyes had a wild look behind them, like I was trying his last nerve.

And maybe I was.

"Come here." His voice was dangerously low.

I walked toward him slowly, suddenly feeling nervous. What if my plan backfired? What if instead of punishing me like last time, he just fired me instead? I swallowed, my mouth suddenly drier than a cotton ball.

I stopped a couple of feet away from him, but he crooked his finger, beckoning me closer. I gulped and complied, moving forward until we were eye to eye, his gaze boring into me. He was so close now that I could smell the fresh scent of his aftershave just inches from my nose.

"What," he said, "Is this?"

He thrust a piece of paper in front of me, and I suppressed a smirk. The copy I'd made of the boardroom minutes was off center, the edge cut off in a way I knew was making him crazy. Mr. Drake was nothing if not a control freak.

"It's the copy you asked for," I said, innocently.

He grimaced before crumpling the copy into a tight ball.

"This is not the standard of work I require, *Isabeau*, and I think you know that. Where the hell is your head today?"

He grabbed my hand, making me jump, and shoved the wad of paper into it.

"Get this out of my sight and do it again. RIGHT, this time!"

I waited another moment, hoping he'd say something else, but he just stared at me like I was an idiot.

"Don't make me repeat myself," he growled, and stood, towering over me.

"Yes, Sir," I said, and high tailed it out of there.

I sighed as I recopied the minutes, feeling the sting of embarrassment coloring my cheeks as I thought about my gorgeous boss. I'd hoped if I provoked him, he'd lose control again and ask me to bend over his desk, like he had just one week ago. It had been one of the hottest experiences of my life, being totally at his mercy as he spanked my ass red and brought me to orgasm... All because I was naughty and needed to be punished.

But where was my punishment now? He said it would never happen again, but I couldn't accept it, not after what had passed between us. I bit my lip anxiously, replaying our interactions over the past few days in my head. He had been nothing but purely professional, if a little gruff at times.

He was still Chase Drake, demanding billionaire CEO, after all, even if he did have one indiscretion with his lowly assistant. Maybe that's all I was to him. A replaceable toy that he would never stoop to sleep with, much less date. Now that he'd had his fun, he'd cast me aside.

Who was I kidding? Maybe he was serious when he said he'd never touch me like that again. Never lose control.

I handed him the fresh copy with his afternoon coffee, and he didn't so much as look at me. My heart clenched in my chest, but I kept my chin high, and my eyes impassive as I backed out and took my spot at my desk.

It was like he'd already forgotten that anything had happened.

And maybe you should, too, Isa. Don't get involved. It was a terrible idea from the start, messing around with the boss.

I sighed and lay my head down on the wood, hoping against hope that the clock would speed up and the day would end. And that maybe, I could forget what happened, too.

***

"Isa…"

I awoke to a gentle hand on my shoulder. For a moment, I didn't know where I was. The room was dim, the lights out, and only the rays of the street light cast a glow through the window. I realized my head was on something hard, and raised up, moaning softly as my back popped. I had a crick in my neck and rubbed it, still groggy and disoriented.

"You fell asleep at your desk."

My eyes widened at the familiar, low voice. Chase Drake was kneeling down next to me, his cufflink gleaming in the beam of light, his face cast in shadow. I knew he was watching me carefully, even though I couldn't see his expression.

"I… I'm sorry… I must be a mess."

My hand flew to my hair, trying desperately to smooth down fly-aways, but it was hopeless. My bun had come undone, my curls spilling down over my shoulder on one side.

He grabbed my wrist, stopping me.

"Isabeau. Stop."

His touch made me shiver, and a feeling of dread welled up inside of me. I couldn't believe I'd fallen asleep here and let him find me like this. This was beyond making a crappy copy or forgetting cream in his coffee. This was inexcusable. I hung my head.

"Look at me."

His voice was almost a whisper, but sounded everything like a command. I raised my eyes as he moved closer, into the light. Instead of the anger I'd expected, his eyes held an unexpected tenderness.

"You look beautiful," he said, smoothing the hair out of my eyes.

I sucked in a breath, unsure how to react. Was I in trouble? Or not?

His hand lingered in my hair, teasing my curls around his fingers. My heart was thumping so loudly, I wondered if he could hear the effect he had on me.

"Mr. Drake?"

He stood abruptly, pulling me up with him.

"It's late. Let me drive you."

"But, I… It's so much trouble."

He eyed me in a strange way. "I know you take the bus, Isa. Surely, they've stopped running by now."

I looked away again. He was just trying to be a good guy, but the fact that I was now his burden because of my slip up was too much.

"You don't have to do that, Mr. Drake. I can get myself home just fine. It's my fault for falling asleep like that. I… I didn't know you'd be working so late."

"*Ms. Willcox*," he said, his tone harsh, but mocking. "If I have to throw you over my shoulder and carry you to my car, I'll do it. I want you home safe, not walking home in the dark to save on cab fare."

My cheeks were burning, shame welling up inside of me. He was worth more than I'd ever see in my lifetime, hell, more than I could imagine, and here I was, poor and alone, without enough money for cab fare. How did he know? And more importantly, what must he think of me?

"So, I was right." He stared down at me frowning, a crease growing on his brow.

I ran a hand over my face and sighed before pulling out of his grip. "I'm fine, Mr. Drake. Really."

I grabbed my purse and made for the elevator, but as soon as I pushed the button, there he was. I felt his presence like a force of nature, larger than life behind me. I didn't turn around, daring myself to stand tall, despite the embarrassment I felt like a sock to the gut.

The doors slid open, and we stepped through together. There was silence on the ride down to the lobby, but I could feel his eyes on me, assessing me coolly like I was a puzzle he was trying to figure out.

When the bell chimed and the doors slid open again, I yelped as I found myself lifted off my feet. Mr. Drake slung me over his shoulder like a sack of potatoes, and I held on for dear life.

"I warned you what would happen if you tried to walk home, Isabeau. I was very clear. You're coming with me, and I won't take 'no' for an answer."

I hung there in shock as he began walking toward the parking lot, bobbing with each step, wondering whether I should laugh or cry. Was my gorgeous boss really carrying me away like a cave man? What the hell?

"I'm fine! Really!" I squeaked, trying not to stare at his sculpted ass, which was conveniently at eye level.

A hard swat came down on my rear, and I gasped.

"That's just about enough of that, Isa. Don't *ever* lie to me."

"But..."

He spanked me again, and my pussy heated, despite the furious blush on my face and the twinge of anger coursing through me at being treated this way. I was a grown woman! I can take care of myself, even if it did mean walking the four miles to my place... in the dark... in heels.

It was my business, and mine alone.

"Enough. One more word out of you before we're in the car, and I'll spank your ass raw right here in public. Is that what you want?"

I opened my mouth to protest, then shut it, sensing the trap.

"Very good," he said, chuckling.

He carried me as if I weighed nothing, moving steadily to the executive lot where his Bentley sat, gleaming black beneath the lonely street lamp. I heard the chirp of his locks springing open, and the rumble of his engine as he remote started it.

Then, the world shifted, and I was being held tightly against him as I regained my feet. His body was hard and warm, and, in that moment, I wanted nothing better than to press myself up against him and let him hold me all night. I pushed away, steadying myself.

"Hop in," he said.

He held the door open for me and grinned, his twin dimples making my insides melt.

I nodded and slid into the supple leather seat, letting him close the door behind me. I repressed a giggle. *You never hear about a caveman opening doors for a lady.* Mr. Drake slid behind the wheel, unbuttoning his Armani suit jacket as he did. I couldn't help but stare for a moment at this man, my boss, who cared so much about me making it home safe.

The door clicked shut, and we were off. We sat in silence for a while as he merged onto the freeway, the lights of the city flickering by like fire flies on a hot summer night. I sat back in the seat, loving the feel of the leather on my skin, before my stomach rumbled loudly, making me wish I could sink into it and disappear.

"Are you hungry?" Mr. Drake glanced over at me and grinned. When I didn't respond, he added, "You can talk now, you know."

I smiled into the darkness. "A bit. I haven't eaten since breakfast."

"I'm starving, too. Hang on. I know a place."

Before I could protest, he was exiting, moving toward downtown, away from my apartment. I realized that I never told him where I lived. Where had he been taking me?

We pulled up to a restaurant whose name I couldn't pronounce, and he opened the car door for me once again before tossing his keys to the valet. Yep. There was a freaking *valet* at this place. I looked down at my work clothes and chewed my lip. Mr. Drake was already at the door, holding it for me, looking at me with a raised eyebrow.

The maitre de smiled and shook Mr. Drake's hand before ushering him to "his table." It was my turn to raise an eyebrow as I looked around the place. The lights were low and candles flickered on every table. The walls were covered in gorgeous polished wood with art work hanging in lighted niches. I'd never been to a restaurant like this, and suddenly, I was glad for the dim lighting. I stuck out like a sore thumb.

I ran my hands through my hair, trying to smooth it out now that it was down, before Mr. Drake caught my hand. His eyes seemed to be looking through me before he pulled my chair out and gestured for me to sit. He sat down before letting me go, his hand lingering on mine.

"Are you uncomfortable here?"

His question caught me off guard. Was I that obvious?

"A little," I said. "I'm not dressed for it." I glanced down at the menu, and swallowed hard. "And I don't think I can afford it," I ended, my voice just above a whisper.

Mr. Drake laughed, and I stared at him in surprise.

"No one cares what you're wearing, Isabeau. You're with me." He leaned in, the angles of his face accentuated by the candlelight. "And when you're with me, it's my treat. I thought that much was obvious."

Relief flooded me, and I sat back with a long exhale. "Thank you, Sir."

There was a strange light in his eyes at the word 'Sir,' but as soon as I saw it, it was gone, and he was leaning comfortably back, looking at the menu. Had I imagined it?

"My pleasure. Now, tell me, Isabeau. Have you ever had foie gras?"

***

At first I'd worried we'd have nothing to talk about, but as dinner wore on, Mr. Drake seemed to delight in introducing me new foods and wines, watching my face intently as I tried them all, and smiling like a kid on Christmas morning when he found something I enjoyed. The bone marrow foam turned out to be delicious instead of disgusting (as I'd feared), and the riesling paired with the crème brulee was the best thing I'd had in years.

He asked about my family, and I told him about my sister and brother back in Oregon, and how I'd been living with my Grandma Rose, taking care of her until she passed away this year.

"That explains why a woman like you was temping. You put your career on hold for her, didn't you?"

I frowned back at him. "What do you mean? 'A woman like me'?"

Is he insulting me? After all this?

"You're a beautiful woman in her mid 20s, Isabeau. College educated, smart, capable. You should have a career. You should be *excelling* in a career. You're not a temp."

I looked down at my hands, twisting my napkin in my lap.

"Sometimes life has other plans, I guess. I hope I didn't *disappoint.*"

My words sounded bitter, but I meant it that way. Who the hell did Mr. Drake think he was? There was nothing wrong with being a temp. I made enough money to have my own, admittedly tiny, place. I paid my bills. I lived my life. Wasn't that enough?

A life like mine will never be enough for some people.

His hand covered mine on the tablecloth, and I looked

up into those green eyes of his.

"I think you misunderstand me. I meant that you can be anything you want to be, and the fact that you sacrificed like that for family is… noble. Your Grandmother was a very lucky woman to have you looking after her. I don't think anyone in my family would ever be that selfless."

I sat in stunned silence, feeling the comforting weight of his hand on mine, realizing I'd misjudged him, even after the kindness he'd shown me tonight.

"Thank you."

Tears had sprung up behind my eyes, and it took all my effort to push them back down. The last thing I needed was for this powerful man to see me cry over dessert. I was just tired, was all. Tired of sacrifice. Tired of second guessing all of my choice. Of trying to be my best every hour of every day.

"Let's get out of here."

***

On the drive home, wine warming me from within combined with the soft murmur of the radio made my eyes heavy. I'd only had a couple of glasses, but I'd sampled several others the sommelier brought over, and had a nice buzz going. Not drunk, but lubricated and comfortable.

Mr. Drake was quiet, seemingly lost in thought as he drove me home. My apartment was a bit of a drive away from the restaurant, and soon I found myself nodding off, try as I might to stay awake.

***

I awoke to strong arms carrying me through a hallway I didn't recognize. I murmured against a soft jacket, and noticed a chandelier out of the corner of my eye. Where the hell was I, and why was I being carried?

The smell of Mr. Drake's aftershave wafted over me, and for a moment, I wanted to pretend I was asleep again, if it meant I could snuggle against him without him stopping me. But I'd raised my head off his muscled shoulder and the moment had passed.

"Where am I?"

"You were sleeping so peacefully, I didn't want to wake you. I brought you to my home instead. I thought you could use the rest."

He stopped and set me down at the entrance to a lavish bedroom. Rich wallpaper gave the room a warm feeling, surrounding the four poster bed covered in lush linens that dominated the room.

"You brought me home with you?"

He gave me a lopsided grin that made my heart do a little flip. "Are you worried I won't be a gentleman?"

I gave him a shy smile. "You have been all night. Why should I doubt you now?"

He showed me the bathroom attached to the guest room, and I stared at the silky white bathrobe hanging in the corner, as well as the toiletries laid out.

"I called ahead while you were sleeping and let the staff know you were coming," he offered, as if he had no idea how strange it sounded to me. "Please. Make yourself comfortable."

I sat on the bed, smoothing my hands over the sheets. They must have been some ridiculous thread count by the luxurious feel of the cotton. Why should I be surprised that even his guest room had the best of the best in it? *He has a staff for God's sake!*

"Thank you, Mr. Drake." I smiled up at him, wondering what this night meant, if anything.

"Please," he said, "Call me Chase when we're not at work."

I smiled up at him and tried the name on for size. "Chase…"

"Goodnight, Isabeau."

26

He closed the door behind him, leaving me with more questions than answers.

***

I awoke in the middle of the night to the sound of footsteps outside my room, then a door creaking open. I rubbed the sleep out of my eyes and climbed out of bed. I pulled on the short silk robe, loving the way it felt against my naked body, and tip toed to the door. If Mr. Drake was up, what was he doing? I glanced at the clock. It was nearly 3 a.m.

I eased the door open and glanced down the hallway. There was a black door at the end of the hall standing ajar, and I heard the sound of ice cubes clinking against glass. I knew I shouldn't snoop, but curiosity burned inside of me. Would one little peek hurt? After all, my host had said to make myself comfortable...

I moved quietly down the hall, padding barefoot on the thick carpet until I was just outside the door. I peered in, my eyes still adjusting. The only light came from a fireplace on the far wall, but I could see Mr. Drake's profile as he sat in a high-backed chair, and slowly raised a glass to his lips. Something lay across his lap, but I couldn't quite make it out. He lowered the glass and raised the whatever it was to his face. It looked like cloth, torn at the bottom...

I gasped out loud as it caught the light. It was my shirt from that day in the office. The one he'd torn undressing me.

Mr. Drake whipped his head around at the sound.

I didn't move in time, and our eyes locked through the crack in the open door.

"What are you doing?" His voice was harsh, and I winced at the tone.

I stepped into the room, tugging the robe tight around my body. "I could ask you the same question."

He looked down at the shirt in his hands, then let it fall to the floor. "You were supposed to be asleep."

The look in his eyes then, a mixture of sadness and regret, made me do something I never thought I'd do. I crossed the room to his chair, took the glass out of his hand and set it on the mantle, before saying exactly what was on my mind—what had been on my mind ever since that day in the office.

"Why won't you punish me any more?"

My voice was soft, almost drowned out by the crackling of the flames, but I knew that he'd heard.

"Isabeau… It isn't that simple."

"What's complicated about it?"

I put my hands on my hips, and noticed his eyes raking over my curves, barely concealed by the thin robe.

"If you don't want me, I understand." My voice cracked a little, despite my wishes, and I looked down, unable to meet his eyes.

He stood, then, towering over me, darkly silhouetted against the flames.

"It's not that. God, Isabeau… you can't know what you do to me."

He moved close, close enough to hold me if that's what he wanted. If so, I wasn't going to stop him.

"Then what is it?" I reached out hesitantly, my fingers trailing along his arm until I reached his hand. He didn't pull away.

"You don't know what you're asking."

"Try me."

There was a moment of tension, so thick I could barely breathe, and then he closed the distance between us, grabbing me roughly, his lips crashing down on mine. His mouth was hot and urgent, making my knees shiver and my pussy heat. I moaned, opening my lips beneath his, and felt a surge of arousal course through me as his tongue met mine, searching, tasting, teasing...

I clutched the front of his shirt, wanting to rip it off, but not sure if it was okay, if it was proper. He broke the kiss, and looked at me like a wild animal, his eyes ravenous. I was afraid and nervous and more turned on than I'd ever been in my life.

"I can smell your need," he growled, and slipped a hand beneath my robe, cupping my sex. "You're on fire for me."

"Oh, God," I whispered. My core was so wet, so ready, and I felt my juices drip down onto his palm.

"Tell me you want this."

It wasn't a question.

"I… I want this."

That was all it took.

He jerked the belt of my robe open and tore it down off my shoulders. The silk whispered at it fell to the ground. His eyes roamed my curves, taking in my round breasts and firm body, my nipples peaking under his gaze. For a moment, I wanted to cover up, to avoid his searching stare, but then he touched me with those strong hands, and all thoughts of shyness disappeared.

He was rough, but gentle lovemaking was the last thing on my mind. He caressed my breasts, stopping to twist and pinch each nipple into a stinging point, making me groan with each jolt of pain. I reached for the buttons of his shirt, but he slapped my hands, unbuttoning it himself and tossing it aside.

His body was exactly as I'd imagined: toned, hard, with a sprinkling of light brown hair across his powerful chest. I wanted to touch him, to take my time, licking my way down to that oh-so-sexy spot where his abs met his hip, but he held my wrists in one hand as he worked his buckle. He drew a condom out of his pocket, then dropped his pants and underwear to the floor.

I gasped when I saw his erection, stiff and huge, the tip already glistening with pre-cum, ready to bury itself between my legs. I squirmed in his grasp, needing him now, wanting him more than I thought was possible. He released my hands just long enough to rip the condom wrapper open and roll it on, then threw my arms around his neck.

"Clasp your hands together, and don't let go.

Understand?"

It was an order, and my body tingled at his commanding tone, ready and eager to please.

"Yes, Sir."

I don't know why I said it, but I was instantly glad I did. The look on his face was one of pure animal lust as I did as he demanded, holding my hands together behind his neck, bracing myself against his broad shoulders.

He picked me up with a growl and impaled me with one hard thrust. I cried out as his thick cock stretched me, filling me to an almost painful degree. There was no foreplay, only this, and it was exactly what I craved.

"Is this what you want?" He gritted in my ear.

I gasped in response as he began pumping in and out of me, his hands supporting my ass, bobbing me up and down on his hot erection. I held on for dear life, feeling helpless as he bucked up into me, hitting me hard with each jerk of his hips.

"Answer me! Did you want this, little temp, when you asked why I don't punish you?"

He dug his fingers into my skin, bruising me, but I didn't care. My body felt like it was on fire, filled with the sensations of this man's violent lovemaking, unlike anything I'd ever experienced. My toes curled behind his back as he drove into me again and again and again.

"Y-yes! Yes!"

My voice was high. Breathless. I felt like I was riding a storm, with each thrust getting me closer and closer to being struck by lightning. He bucked into me over and over, and time seemed to stand still as I succumbed to his will, trusting him to hold me as he drove into me again and again.

Then, suddenly, Mr. Drake unclasped my arms from his neck and grabbed my waist, flipping me over. I yelled in surprise as my feet hit the ground and he bent me over his ottoman, my ass sticking up high in the air. He jerked my hands behind my back and held my wrists together again.

"You call me Sir when you're with me like this.

Understand?"

His hand came down hard on one ass cheek, and I yelped at the sharp jolt of pain.

"Yes!"

He hit me again on the same spot, making me moan into the cushion. My pussy ached to be filled by him again; the sweet burn amplifying my need.

"What did I just say? Are you deaf, little temp?"

His hand came down again and again, the sound of flesh hitting flesh reverberating throughout the room.

"I'm sorry, Sir! I understand, Sir!"

I could almost hear him smile behind me, but before I could turn and look, he thrust into me once more. I wailed mindlessly as he began fucking me, harder and harder, faster and faster, taking me then and there like I was his to use and always had been. He pulled my wrists, making me arch my back, helpless to resist the onslaught of his body slamming into mine.

When one hand snaked around my hips and pinched my clit hard, I screamed, the bite of sensation taking me right to the edge, his hard cock taking me tumbling over. I fell apart beneath him, moaning as I convulsed around him again and again, milking him even as he railed into me.

He released my wrists and gripped my ass as he pumped into me once, twice, three more times, abusing the already tender flesh. He groaned behind me, and I sighed as I felt him cumming, his cock twitching inside of me as my pussy gripped it, still pulsing from the strength of my orgasm.

"Good, girl," he said, catching his breath above me. "Good girl…"

***

I lay draped over the ottoman for a minute or two, feeling like all of my bones had been replaced with rubber bands, before I pushed myself up and looked around. Mr.

Drake expertly knotted the condom and tossed it in the trash, then retrieved the silk robe for me.

"Thank you," I said, and we both knew I wasn't talking about the robe.

He smiled down at me, his dimples breathtaking in the flickering firelight.

"Is this really what you want, Isabeau? I'm not a gentle man. I never have been."

I put a hand on my backside, feeling the sweet pain where he'd struck me, and bit my lip.

"Yes. I want this. I want *you*."

I'd never been so blunt before, but Mr. Drake brought out a different side of me. A bolder version of me who admitted what she craved, who said what she felt. Even so, I don't think I would have been able to stand it if he didn't want me in the same way.

He gathered me in his arms and pressed a hot kiss to my lips.

"I've wanted you since the first day I saw you. When I called you 'mouse,' there was a fire in your eyes, but I could tell you longed for someone to trust. Someone to take control. But Isabeau… there's so much more, and I need to know that you're ready. That you do trust me, if we're going to continue."

I didn't understand. What else was there? What was he keeping from me?

"I have something to show you."

He reached into the shadows by the fireplace. I heard a mechanism *click*, then the grinding sound of gears shuddering to life. A small door opened in the brick, swinging inwards into blackness. Mr. Drake hit a switch inside the door, and a secret room was illuminated in soft, orange light.

My mouth dropped open. The room was huge, and looked like something out of a gothic fantasy. A huge black structure leaned against the far wall in the shape of an X, with piles of rope and chain next to it, along with various odd looking stools, benches, and what looked like a leather swing hanging from the ceiling. Dark wooden shelves displayed a variety of dildos, handcuffs and metal bars that made me shiver from head to toe just looking at them.

Another case held whips and riding crops.

"This is my dungeon. My greatest secret. I am a Dom by nature, which means that my lovers must enjoy submission. Bondage. Pleasure tinged with pain."

I gaped at the contents of the hidden room, emotions warring within me. Fear mixed with arousal as my eyes wandered over all of the devices and restraints. Could I do this? Did I *want* to do this? Could I be the lover that Mr. Drake needed?

"Isabeau. Do you trust me?"

I looked up into the green eyes of the man who'd just given me the greatest sex of my life, the man who made my body tingle just by looking at me, and found myself lost for words. This was a defining moment of my life, and the gravity of it stole my breath away.

Did I trust this man enough to submit?

His eyes, usually so full of confidence were darkened by doubt, and I realized he was just as afraid as I was. Afraid that I'd say 'no.' Afraid that I'd leave.

I took his hand in mine.

"I trust you."

He smiled, and pulled me close.

"Then, Isabeau, I have so much to show you."

3 AT HIS COMMAND

Have you ever had one of those moments where something so strange and fantastic is happening to you, that you wonder if you're dreaming? One of those moments that is so surreal, so unlike anything in your ordinary life that you're positive it's a fantasy? But then you pinch yourself. The pain grounds you, and you realize it's really happening.

Your life is changing forever.

This is exactly how I felt as Mr. Drake led me into his secret dungeon and showed me what he had in store for me.

For a few minutes, he let me wander through the room, touching and exploring, asking myself which things I'd like to try. He watched from the doorway, wearing only his silk boxers, a knowing grin on his handsome face.

I picked up a pair of wrist restraints, feeling the suppleness of the leather, longing for the feel of being helpless before this powerful man. I ran my hands over the tails of a flog, then picked up a crop, wondering what it would feel like, laying into me when I was bent over, crying out beneath Mr. Drake's skillful blows.

The cross intrigued me the most, and I ran my hands over its dark surface before turning back to the man watching me closely.

"What is this thing?"

"It's called a St. Andrews cross. If we decided to play with it, I'd lash your wrists to the top two restraints, and your ankles to the bottom two, leaving you spread wide and vulnerable, unable to resist whatever I wanted to do to you."

I shivered, imagining the kind of things he might do when I was bound and naked before him, stretched and ready.

He stepped closer, looming over me.

"Would you like that, Isabeau? Would you like to be helpless to resist while I bring you orgasm after orgasm, denying you what you really want until you are begging to be filled by my cock?"

My eyes almost rolled back in my head from his words alone.

"Yes... Sir."

I wanted it more than anything.

"Then get some rest. Tomorrow, you're mine to do with as I please."

I groaned at his words. "But what about work?"

"Isabeau," he said, grinning down at me. "Tomorrow's Saturday."

***

When I woke, I noticed that my clothes were folded on the trunk on the foot of my bed , with a note sitting on top in an elegant hand.

I have business in the city to attend to, but will return as soon as I can. Please make yourself comfortable. My house is your house while you stay.

I can't wait to see you, little temp.

I read the note over and over again before holding it to my lips. I couldn't believe this was happening. The dream was real, and suddenly, I felt like a very naughty version of Cinderella, living with my kinky Prince Charming.

What's the first thing a princess to do? I wondered, then grinned. *She'd explore the castle, of course!*

I hadn't gotten a good look at my surroundings the night before, but now as I pushed the door open and padded down the hall in my bare feet, I couldn't help but be overwhelmed. Mr. Drake's home was lushly furnished with thick, soft carpets cushioning my steps, and gorgeous artwork displayed in every room. I examined one painting to see if it was a print, but brushstrokes were visible in the lamplight, as clear as day. An original. How much money did he spend on something as simple as decorating?

My one Ikea print hanging over my bed seemed down right sad in comparison. Considering that was my idea of a splurge item when I moved in said a lot about the difference between our two worlds. Suddenly, I felt very small, and very out of place.

The house was enormous, and it took me awhile to find my way down a back stairwell and into the kitchen. A stocky blonde woman looked up from behind the granite counter top and raised a sharp eyebrow at me.

"Miss, those are the stairs the staff uses. Guests use the grand staircase."

I blushed, my face feeling hotter than the noonday sun. "I… I'm sorry. I didn't know."

In fact, I'd forgotten there *was* a staff. The chef nodded curtly at me, and went back to chopping vegetables. I sat down awkwardly on a stool by the counter and wondered what do to next. My stomach growled.

"May I make you something, Miss? An omelet? Or perhaps a crepe?"

I smiled at her. This was all too weird. "Please make me whatever is your favorite."

She grinned back, her icy exterior warming at my words. "Right away, Miss."

We chatted while she worked, and I soon learned that

Katja had worked for Mr. Drake since he left college, leaving his father's household for his. When I finally tried the savory crepe she'd made, my eyes rolled back in my head.

"This may be the best thing I've ever had," I said, groaning.

The older woman beamed at me.

"Danke."

I attempted to pry information about my sexy and mysterious boss from her between bites, but she kept her words cheerfully vague. It seemed she didn't know much about his personal life at all. He usually sent the staff home early after they'd prepared dinner, preferring to serve his guests himself.

"Although he hasn't brought a beautiful young lady such as yourself home in quite some time," she said, her hands on her chef's apron. "And a shame, too! None of them have ever complimented my cooking."

"That's a crime," I said, finishing my last bite and sighing.

"Mr. Drake should be home any moment. Would you please follow me?"

I jumped as a gravelly, male voice interrupted our talk. A silver-haired butler stood behind me, holding a black, wooden box in his hands and looking grave.

"Uh… of course, Mister…?"

The man gave a deep bow. "Mr. Daniels, my lady. If you would please follow me?"

I thanked Katja, and followed him through the winding halls of the house until we were outside of Mr. Drake's study, where I'd found him holding my torn shirt the night before. I tingled with anticipation, wondering when he would appear, and what he'd do to me in his dungeon when he did.

Mr. Daniels set the box on a low table by the fire.

"I've been instructed to tell you to please put on the contents of the box, and wait here for the master's arrival."

I nodded, my pulse thudding in my ears, adrenaline coursing through me. What had he left me?

"Yes, of course," I stuttered. "Thank you very much, Mr. Daniels."

"Miss."

He bowed low again and saw himself out of the room. The door snapped shut behind him.

Curious, I rushed to open the box. Inside was a crimson garter belt and matching bra, as well as a couple of devices and a bottle that made me blush. There was also another note in Mr. Drake's handwriting.

Wear these items and nothing else.
The black plug goes in back, and the white in front.
I expect you ready and waiting for me, Isabeau.
Do not disappoint me.

I stared down at the box, my mouth hanging open. The idea of being filled completely intrigued me, but I admit, I was also more than a little nervous. I'd never had anything in my ass before, and even though the plug before me was small, I didn't know how it would feel. Would it hurt?

I slowly removed my clothes, folding them carefully and setting them aside before wiggling into the embroidered garter and lacy black stockings. It felt strange to be wearing all this without panties covering me, but also naughty, leaving me feeling deliciously exposed. I slipped the bra on, and then picked up the bottle of lube, biting my lip.

I got on my knees and took a deep breath, reaching behind me to slide it into position. *Here goes nothing.*

When the plug pushed against my pucker, I gasped at the feel of the cold gel, then at the sensation of my ring of muscle wrapping around it, accepting it into my body. It stung a little as I adjusted to the tapered silicone inside me, making me squirm on the carpet. It felt so wrong doing something like this, but the feeling made my sex heat and my body tingle all over.

If my conservative family ever knew I did anything like this, they'd each have a heart attack before calling my pastor.

I smiled and reached for the delicate, white vibrator. It was egg shaped and slipped easily inside of me as my walls squeezed around it. There was no button or anything that I could see, but the feeling of these two toys rubbing together through the thin membrane of skin separating them was almost too much to take.

I waited there, on my knees, half expecting Mr. Drake to burst in at any moment. I was so ready for him, I ached, longing for him to take me and show me something I'd never experienced before. To take me deeper into his world.

The sound of a key scraping in a lock made me spin around to face the door. Suddenly embarrassed, I covered my privates, in case it was Mr. Daniels coming back to check on me. The lock snapped and I could hear footfalls moving away from the door. I furrowed my brow, frowning before it finally hit me. I was locked in!

I ran to the door and tried the knob, swearing under my breath when it didn't move. What the hell was going on?

I yelped as the plug in my ass and the vibrating egg both buzzed to life, making me rock on my feet and clutch the door knob for support. My body felt like it was on fire, the powerful vibrations making me gasp for air. I hadn't touched any buttons, but they were both pulsing in time, making my clench around them.

Just as quickly as they started, they stopped, and I stood panting, trying to catch my breath. I reached between my legs, looking for some kind of switch so I could control these things, but as I did, a voice resonated from a speaker in the ceiling.

"Hands at your sides, Isabeau."

I gasped, but did as I was told. "Mr. Drake?"

"Very good, my little temp. I love how quickly you obey me. You deserve a reward."

The butt plug and dildo buzzed to life again, and I

doubled over, groaning. The vibrations in my ass were driving me wild in a way I'd never experienced. It was intense. Too intense.

"Please..."

The vibrations stopped.

"You look beautiful, Isa. I knew that color would suit you. Not like those horrid pastels you usually wear. You're too wild for that. A very bad girl trapped inside a good girl's clothes."

I straightened up again, my hands and my sides and looked around, wondering how he could see me. There were no windows, and the door was shut tight behind me. I spied a shining black dot nestled at the foot of a bust on the mantle. A camera. Bingo.

"Before we play today, there are some matters to discuss. Some ground rules, if you will."

"What kind of rules?"

There was a low chuckle. "Eager, aren't we? Well, first, you are always to address me as 'Sir' when we play. I am your master, and you are my dirty little slave girl, understood? I own you when you're in my dungeon, Isabeau."

I trembled at his words, feeling my thighs growing slick with my own arousal.

"But my part of that exchange is my promise to keep you safe, always, at all times. You give me your trust, and I earn every second of it. That's the deal."

I nodded, the weight of his words settling over me. I would have to trust him completely, but the thought of him dominating me, protecting me even as he caused me pain... It made me moan quietly, and move my fingers to my pussy.

"Bad girl, Isabeau! I'm not done explaining."

He gave me a quick pulse from the vibrators, just enough to shock me. I grinned and put my hands back at my sides.

"Are you willing to put yourself in my hands? Will you be my little slave, Isa?"

I sighed, enchanted by the thought of being in his hands, bending to his every whim.

"Yes, Sir…"

There was a weighty pause, and I pictured him smiling, wherever he was, looking me over, seeing the effect he already had on me.

"The next rule is perhaps the most important. If I go too far, or if you want things to stop for any reason, you need a word to say to put a halt to things. A safe word. If we're playing a game where 'stop' doesn't mean 'stop,' you use that word, and I stop immediately. Do you understand?"

I nodded, wondering what I could possibly use, but feeling comfort at the thought of that fail safe.

"I do."

"Think of your word, and then we can begin."

Buzzing ripped through my body, making my knees buckle. I fell to the carpet, bracing myself against the ottoman as my core squeezed around the pulsing toys.

"Once you've cum twice for me, I'll let you out, and we'll hear that safe word."

"What?!" I gasped. He wanted me to cum *twice?* Here and now? While he watched?

My cheeks burned, but the vibrations were making it hard to feel anything else, including shame. My whole world narrowed to the knowledge that he was watching me, controlling me. The pattern of vibration changed, pulsing twice, then once, slow, then fast, and I knew he was playing my body like an instrument from afar, willing me to cum for him.

He didn't have to wait long.

The pulsing in my ass against the egg in the front made me come apart, wailing on my back, legs squeezed together as my body convulsed. I shuddered, my thighs trembling, my clit overly sensitive, but the vibrations kept on.

And just when I thought I couldn't take it any longer, Mr. Drake amped up the power.

My screams echoed off the walls, filling my ears.

***

I lay limp in Mr. Drake's strong arms as he carried me into the dungeon, sweaty and wrung out from my orgasms.

The door closed behind us, and he whispered in my ear. "What's your safe word?"

"Ramen," I said, grinning against his shoulder, thinking of the day he'd ripped my shirt off after I spilled ramen noodles down my front.

His low laugh made his chest rumble against my cheek. "Ramen, it is."

He stopped in front of a swing suspended from the ceiling by heavy duty metal hooks, the leather straps on the side ending in cuffs that I eyed with longing. Mr. Drake lifted me into it as if I weighed no more than a child, and went to work securing my arms over my head, then moving down to spread my legs wide, strapping my ankles in with the supple leather.

I was opened up before him, nothing hidden from his view. I saw the hunger burning in his eyes as his gaze raked over my body. He undid his silver tie and slid it to the floor, then unbuttoned his shirt with surgical precision as I watched, just as hungry as he was. I couldn't wait to see that muscled chest of his—his fit body beaded with sweat as he bent over me...

I licked my lips as his shirt fell beside his tie, and waited for him to undo his belt buckle. Instead, he reached for my bra, and roughly pulled my breasts out of the lace, displaying them on top of the cups. He leaned over and rolled each nipple between his fingers, pinching them hard until I gasped.

"Do you like that, little slave?"

I exhaled hard at his words, my pussy heating below. "Y-yes, Sir."

He pinched them one last time, then leaned back, assessing his work. My nipples were erect, the tips red and puffy from his attentions.

"Good girl."

He disappeared to one side, and I craned my head to try

to follow him, squinting into the dim light of the dungeon. Then, his hand closed around my throat from behind, making me tense with fear.

"I'm going to show you a whole new world, little girl," he rasped, making me tremble.

Something black and leather caressed my shoulder, then moved down, sliding over my chest. Glancing down I saw it was the end of one of the riding crops, and I tensed, my heart hammering in my chest. Mr. Drake moved it slowly downward, tracing the curves of each of my breasts, holding my neck so I could watch each movement.

"A world where you belong to *me*."

He flicked the crop, slapping the leather down sharply onto one nipple. I screamed at the sharp sting, and his hand tightened on my throat.

"I use you as I please. I give you pain when it pleases me, and pleasure only when you deserve it. Do you think you deserve it now, slave?"

His wrist flicked again, snapping the head of the crop against the soft tissue of my breast. I whimpered, tears burning my eyes.

"I... I don't know, Sir."

"Unacceptable answer."

He moved to my side, looming over me, and ran the crop lower, toying with me, tracing the curve of my hip before tracing the inside of my thigh. I felt so helpless, unable to move, waiting for the next blow to fall, wondering what it would feel like, and fearing it all the same.

"When I ask you a question, I want either a 'yes, Sir' or a 'no, Sir.' 'I don't know' is not an option, Isabeau."

The crop whipped down, sending blazing pain spidering over my inner thigh. I pulled against the cuffs, writhing beneath him, unable to cover myself. Despite the pain, my body was heating more and more with each blow, my sex dripping against the edge of the swing.

"Understood?"

"Yes, Sir!"

Tears trailed down my cheeks, but I'd never felt so alive. My body was on fire, sensations sharper than they'd ever been before, lighting up my nerves. The leather against my back felt decadent, the cuffs pleasantly snug, the red marks on my breast and leg sensual and obscene.

"Do you deserve pleasure, slave?"

"No, Sir…"

The crop traced the spread lips of my pussy, making me moan. My feet strained against the cuffs, but whether I wanted to close my legs or spread them wider, I wasn't sure.

"And why is that, pray tell?"

"I… I haven't pleased you yet."

I thought about how badly I wanted to take him in my mouth, to run my lips and tongue over him. To feel him shudder inside of me as I gave him release. As I made him happy.

He chuckled darkly. The crop tapped lightly on my clit, making me purse my lips and bite back a yell. Jolts of awareness surged through me, pain and pleasure mixing until they were indistinguishable. All I felt was the intensity, and my body reacted, making me shiver.

"But you have pleased me, slave. You came for me as directed, and you followed my instructions. Your training is going very well so far."

The crop tapped my lower lips in a staccato rhythm, making me wail as the burning washed over me once again.

"In fact, I think you've earned a reward--my cock ramming deep inside your sweet little pussy. Would you like that, slave?"

I wanted it so badly, I could barely speak. "*Please*," I whispered. "Sir."

Mr. Drake grinned, the hunger in his eyes making him look wolfish, like a predator eyeing his prey. He leaned to the side, then came back with a thin chain in his hands, with a small silver clamp on each end.

He pinched my nipples again, making me moan, before attaching a clamp to each one. I cried out as they snapped into place, and bit my lip at the way they felt—each one creating a sensual ache that made me need him even more desperately.

"You look so beautiful like this," he breathed, moving between my legs. "Bound for me. Chained…"

I heard his zipper lower, and wished I could reach down, to stroke him to hardness and guide him inside me. Instead I stared into his piercing green eyes as he positioned himself, and gasped in pleasure as I felt his tip pushing into me, stretching me wide for him.

He slammed into me, then, sheathing himself inside me in one sure stroke. I cried out as he reached out and gripped the chain attached to my sensitive nipples, yanking sharply as he began moving in and out. I screamed at the pain, then panted, my eyes closing at the intensity of sensation coursing through me.

This was like nothing I'd ever felt before, and with each pump of Mr. Drake's, my master's, rod inside of me, I felt fireworks going off behind my eyes, making me soar in sparks of desire, the flames ensconcing me, burning the old me as the new one rose from the ashes, terrifying and beautiful.

A new woman. A new beginning. A new Isabeau.

"Yes, slave. Take it all. All that I have to give you," he growled, pulling the swing back onto him, using me like a toy. His toy.

He jerked the chain again, and I wailed like an animal, my inhibitions flowing out of me like water as he took control. I let go, giving myself over as he fucked me harder, savoring each moment, each different texture of lovemaking, each sting and pulse, each jolt and caress.

I squeezed around my master, already on the edge again, unbelieving even as I accepted it was possible with this man. Everything was possible.

"Cum for me, Isabeau," he commanded, and released the nipple clamps, creating a wave of aching pain as the blood rushed back.

I did as I was told, shaking with the force of it as my

pleasure crashed over me, sweeping me away, rocking my body as it rocked my mind, tearing away all of my old notions of what sex could be, should be.

I heard him groan, and felt him cumming inside of me, the thought bringing me to another high as I knew I'd finally pleased him. My boss. My master.

I must have blacked out for a moment, but when my eyes fluttered open again, he was there, rubbing my wrists in his strong hands as he undid the cuffs, then moved to my ankles, releasing me. He lifted me gently out of the sling, and carried me to a corner of the room covered in soft pillows. He knelt down, then pulled me into his lap. He kissed my hair and neck, then trailed soft kisses across my forehead and cheeks.

"How do you feel?" he said, his voice full of concern.

I smiled sleepily and leaned against him, overcome by the feelings bubbling up inside of me.

"Good. Different... but good."

"That's my girl."

He tilted my head up and kissed my lips softly, making me melt at the tenderness of it, after what we'd just done.

"I was worried you might change your mind about being with me. Like this."

I looked into his eyes. The uncertainty there startled me.

"Of course not."

He kissed my hair again, then set me down.

"Wait here, little temp. I have something for you."

I leaned back against the pillows, feeling tired and sore and delicious all over, the soft ache between my legs and in the peaks of my breasts sweet reminders of his touch.

He returned and knelt before me, handing me a black, leather box. I raised an eyebrow.

"Open it. They're for you, if you want them."

I lifted the lid, and gasped at what lay within. There was a thin, black leather collar and beside it a gorgeous platinum choker, dotted with winking diamonds, a tiny charm hanging from the front in the shape of a lock. It must have been worth a fortune.

I had no words.

"Every good slave needs a collar, Isabeau. If you're to be mine, you'll need one when we play… and one to wear to the office." He looked deeply into my eyes. "Will you accept these? Will you be mine?"

My mind spun, the magnitude of the diamonds making me feel uncomfortable, but the gesture making me tingle from head to toe. I'd never owned anything so precious by far, but could I accept such a lavish gift? And if I did, what would it mean?

Something told me this was far more than just going steady.

I'd be collared. His slave. His woman. *His.*

But for how long?

The office gossip came back to me, the words of the ladies around the water cooler echoing in my mind. *None of his assistants lasts long. He's impossible to please.*

If I accepted his offer, how long would it be before he was sick of me? Would he just fire me out of hand like the assistant before me? Or was this something special? Different?

I looked down at the collars and back at Mr. Drake, the man who was slowly stealing my heart.

Could I do this? Could I let him be my master? Could I wear his collar?

He stared back at me, expecting an answer.

But at that moment, I didn't have one.

4 AT HIS INSISTENCE

"I'm waiting, Isabeau."

I glanced down at the diamond choker, sparkling even in the dim light of Mr. Drake's dungeon, perfectly juxtaposed with the black, leather collar sitting next to it on a velvet cushion.

How could I accept such a gift? And could I give myself to him when he might ditch me for a newer model at any moment? What made me, Isabeau Willcox, different from all the rest?

I looked into his eyes, so intense, willing me to speak, to say 'yes' to his proposal. I could tell my silence was grating on him, even as he held me close, the sweat from our lovemaking mingling on our naked bodies.

"I can't."

The look in his eyes made me cringe.

"At least... not yet."

His eyes flashed dangerously, and he stood, pushing me off him onto my feet. My bones still felt like Jell-O from the earth-shattering sex we'd just had, but now I wanted to cover up, to hide from his accusing stare.

"Tell me why."

His voice was deep and dangerous as he set the box aside, closing it with a snap. This was obviously not what he'd planned on happening, and it visibly chafed him. Mr. Drake was nothing if not a control freak.

"I…"

I reached a hand out to touch him, to comfort him, but pulled it back on second thought.

"I'm not sure. At the office, they say you go through assistants like Kleenex."

My hand darted to my mouth. I hadn't meant to just come right out and say it! I didn't mean to blurt out what made me hesitate, when all I wanted was to run into his arms and say I'd be his.

Damn it, Isabeau!

He moved so fast, I didn't have time to think. His hand was on my throat, his thumb caressing the hollow of my neck in a way that made my blood boil and fear course through me like a drug.

"So that's it, is it? You don't trust me? Even after tonight?" He shook his head, pulling me closer.

I gasped in his grip.

"Answer me when I ask you a question, Isabeau."

"I do… it's just…"

I couldn't think with his hand on me like this, his face just inches from mine.

"Just what?"

"What makes me so different?"

I looked him square in the eyes, and blushed as I felt the tears stinging my own. *Don't let him see you cry. Get yourself together.*

The thought of giving myself over to him only to be discarded was more than I could bear. This whole thing felt like a dream, and maybe it was only that, and my time was always limited. But was it worth it if it would only end in heartbreak?

Mr. Drake's hand remained on my throat, caressing me gently, but reminding me of who was in the position of power. His other hand stroked my face, brushing my hair back, the touch making me tingle. Something behind his eyes changed as he looked at me. If I didn't know better, I'd say they were tinged with sadness.

"You really don't know how special you are, do you?"

For a moment, his words took my breath away.

Then he turned, leaving me standing naked and alone in his dungeon. I froze, stunned, for a few seconds, before hurrying after him, through the concealed door and out into the study. I called after him down the hallway.

"Wait! Aren't I sleeping with you tonight?"

He turned, and I could tell he was smirking even in the shadows. "I'll share my bed when you wear my collar."

With that, he walked away, leaving me alone with my regret.

***

In the morning, another note was waiting for me, this time informing me that a car was outside, ready to take me anywhere I wished to go.

Rich man brush off, I thought, frowning. I'd definitely pissed him off by not accepting his offer out of hand. Would he want to see me again? Or was I Miss Self Fulfilling Prophecy? I covered my face with my hands. How could I have been so stupid?

Mr. Drake was everything I wanted in a man, and several things I'd never even considered, but now couldn't live without. Gorgeous, confident, self-made, and dominant in a way that made things feel simpler. Calmer. Safer.

I chewed my lip, turning that thought over in my mind. Why would I feel safe around someone so dangerous? Why would I feel safe with a man who liked the things that he did? Who enjoyed inflicting pain? Imposing his will?

His words from the other night came back to me; what he'd said right before he'd shown me his darkest secret.

"I could tell you longed for someone to trust. Someone to take control."

Was he right? Did I long for someone to take control?

To let me off the hook for just a little while?

I thought of those years I spent taking care of my family, making sure we had food on the table, and then caring for Grandma Rose until she passed away. I'd always had the weight of the world on my shoulders, but now that I was on my own, I felt lost. Maybe giving up the reins was exactly what I needed.

Maybe it would help me discover how to take care of myself. To put my own needs first, even as I surrendered to *his*.

Mr. Drake's...

The thought of pleasing him, of being his to command, of doing as he demanded, filled me with longing. But had I screwed things up before they had a chance to get going? Would Mr. Drake still want me after last night?

I dressed quickly and followed Mr. Daniels to the waiting Rolls Royce. I raised an eyebrow at the choice of vehicle, then slid into the back with a muttered "thank you." I couldn't believe I was going back to my crappy apartment in this thing, but I supposed I'd have to get used to it if I was really going to pursue this.

By the time I reached home, I'd made up my mind: It was worth the risk. I would be Mr. Drake's slave. I would give him control when we were alone, and do my best to please him.

That is, if he'd still have me.

***

The next day I arrived at the office in my best red dress and high heels, ready to declare myself his, only to find that Mr. Drake was out for the day. I drummed my fingernails on the desk, willing the time to pass, but the clock seemed to be rigged to move at half speed. If I didn't need the money, I would have left then and there to go find him, but I couldn't risk losing a day's wages.

I fidgeted as I worked through a pile of transcriptions, stopping frequently to daydream about what I would say to him once I saw him again. I mumbled the words to myself at my desk in the empty corridor outside the executive office, practicing.

"I'm sorry, Sir. I let my fear get the best of me. I do trust you, and I want to do this. To be with you…"

It sounded so stiff, but I'd never been good at voicing my emotions.

"This is the best thing that's ever happened in the whole of my boring-ass life," I said, sighing. "I can't chicken out now."

The bell on the elevator chimed, and I sat up straight, smoothing my hair down in case it was Mr. Drake returning.

A bike messenger stepped out and made his way to my desk, holding out a manila envelope with one word scrawled across it. *Isabeau.*

"I was told to leave this with you," he said.

Curious, I took it from him. "Do you know who it's from?"

He shrugged, looking bored. "I just go where I'm told, lady. Some guy had me waiting in the lobby all morning to deliver this as just the right time. Weirdo."

He made for the elevator without looking back. I waited until the doors slid shut behind him before tearing the envelope open. I pulled out a note written in an elegant hand on Mr. Drake's personal stationary.

I knew you'd change your mind, my little temp. Stay with me tonight.

But first, pick yourself up some new clothes. A car is waiting outside to take you to the stores I prefer. You'll need a cocktail dress, shoes and lingerie.

I opened my mouth, wanting to protest, even though no

one was around, then smiled as I read the last line.

Do as you're told, or you'll get more than a spanking.

He knew me so well.

I raised an eyebrow. He knew me *too* well. How did he know I'd changed my mind about being his?

I peered around me, scrutinizing everything on my desk for the first time. Then, I spotted it—a Drake & Smith pen holder stood nestled between my stapler and computer monitor. A black camera lens winked up at me from the middle of the ampersand.

That sick bastard has been spying on me! I wondered if there was a microphone in place as well and shook my head. Suddenly, I grinned, and reached for my post-it-notes. I scrawled a quick note, and held it up to the camera.

Your wish is my command, SIR.

I blew a kiss, then covered the camera with the yellow post-it. I giggled, imagining his face contorting in annoyance as the visual cut out. I was definitely going to be punished for that little stunt later. But for now, I had more important things to do.

I turned the envelope over, and a credit card slid out onto my desk. It was an American Express Black Card, made of titanium, and it clunked as it hit the wood. I gasped. I'd heard about these, but never seen one in real life. They were invitation-only and as exclusive as it gets… and here I was holding one in my hand.

I picked my jaw up off the floor and headed for the elevator. It would be a shame to keep Mr. Drake waiting.

***

When the Rolls pulled up in front of the first store, I couldn't believe my eyes. This was a section of town I'd never shopped in, for obvious reasons. There was a Tiffany's next to a Giorgio Armani, and several boutiques with French names that seemed more than a little intimidating. I stepped out of the car, and gave the driver a nervous glance.

"You'll be fine, Miss Willcox," he said, his smile making his eyes crinkle. "The boutique is just up ahead. They're waiting for you."

I nodded and mouthed a "thank you." My mouth was too dry for words at that moment. What was I doing? I didn't belong in a place like this, wearing a dress that I'd purchased on sale at the Gap. It was humiliating.

I gripped my purse so tightly my knuckles were turning white, feeling queasy about the credit card inside. How much did I dare put on there? It was all just too weird. I felt uncomfortable just thinking about spending someone else's money on something so frivolous as clothing.

I forced myself to walk, putting one foot in front of the other until I was at the door of the boutique. But before I could touch the door, it swung open, and a beautiful older woman handed me a glass of champagne.

"You must be Miss Willcox," she said, beaming at me. Her icy blonde hair was swept into a classic up-do; her clothing impeccable and of the finest quality.

"My girls and I are going to take excellent care of you today. If you'll follow me, Mr. Drake has laid some items out for you to choose from."

I sipped the champagne, letting the cool bubbles play on my tongue. *Of course he has.*

I smiled. He's taken care of everything. *I should have suspected as much.*

***

Four hours later, the Rolls Royce pulled up in front of the Drake mansion, coming to a stop in front of the huge wooden doors. I fussed with the strap on my new sky-high black heels, wrapped around my freshly pedicured feet. I felt ridiculous in this dress, but it was my favorite out of all the choices laid out by Mr. Control Freak himself. All of them were exquisitely made, not to mention short and revealing, but something about this one had mesmerized me as soon as I held it up to the light.

Metallic silk draped low in the front, hugging my hips enough to flatter, and dropping dangerously low in back, baring enough skin to make me blush. I'd never been one for slinky dresses or showing off my body. Added together with the $500 heels and I felt completely out of sorts, like a pig in lipstick.

Hopefully I didn't look too ridiculous.

Mr. Drake's butler held the door for me as I entered, and I smiled shyly at him.

"You look lovely, if I may say so, Miss Willcox."

My cheeks heated, and I knew I was blushing. "Thank you, Mr. Daniels."

He seemed sincere, which made me feel braver, but I still had my boss to face. Would I impress, and would it be enough to make up for my earlier mistrust?

"Please follow me," he said, and escorted me through the winding halls and up the stairs, to the lavish guest suite I'd used before.

On the bed was a box, gift wrapped in silver paper. Before I could ask any questions, Mr. Daniels bowed himself out, shutting the door behind him. I sat on the bed and carefully opened the paper, folding it and setting it aside. I always ripped through wrapping paper on Christmas and birthdays, but here, in Mr. Drake's home, it seemed wrong, somehow. Sloppy.

I lifted the lid of the wooden box inside and gasped.

There was the vibrating egg again, and, of course, a note accompanying it. When was I going to see the man behind the curtain?

Please do me the honor of being my date at the party I'm throwing this evening. There will be investors coming, and I know having you on my arm will be my lucky charm.

However, you still need to be punished for doubting me. Put this in before you join me in the foyer.

And Isabeau? I expect you on your best behavior tonight. No squirming allowed.

I ran my hands over my temples. He could *not* be serious! He wanted me to wear this sex toy while he paraded me in front of investors and party guests. His business career could be on the line on a night like tonight, and he wanted to play games...

But I had to admit, the thought of wearing this in front of a room full of strangers made my body tingle and my pulse race. It would be a secret only the two of us knew about, and if I judged him right, he'd have the control to flip the switch and turn it on whenever he pleased, controlling my body beneath everyone's noses, and no one the wiser.

Unless I screwed up and let my feelings show.

I bit my lip, fear and excitement warring within me. I'd show him just how cool I could be. I wouldn't disappoint him.

***

I took a deep breath at the top of the winding main staircase, steeling myself.

You can do this, Isabeau. Just breathe.

I held onto the handrail and moved down the steps carefully, my core squeezing around the egg beneath my new lace panties. I still couldn't believe I was doing this, but the thought of Mr. Drake somewhere below, waiting to turn me on was almost too much to bear. I felt like I was on fire for him, and I hadn't even seen him yet.

I turned the corner, and the foyer opened up beneath me. Guests in expensive suits and glamorous dresses mingled below, diamonds catching the light on necks and wrists everywhere I looked.

I wanted to stop walking. I wanted to turn around and retreat to the safety of my room, or maybe lock myself in the bathroom and climb out the window. I felt like such an imposter wearing these clothes, trespassing on this life… Would they be able to tell? Would just one look give me away?

I hesitated, my hand hovering over the banister, before I saw him. He was standing near the bar, a glass of scotch in one hand, the other tucked nonchalantly in his jacket pocket, talking to several gentlemen. Intense, green eyes locked on mine, and for a moment, everything else melted away.

The egg roared to life inside me.

I pressed my lips together, my whole body tensing as I tried to retain my composure. I knew he was watching, waiting to see if I'd be able to obey him. If I'd be able to hold onto my dignity despite what he was making me feel.

I squeezed my thighs together, took a deep breath, and kept walking, my chin held high. At the bottom of the steps, the pulsing stopped, and I let go a sigh of relief as I saw Mr. Drake smile, his dimples making me tingle all over again. He downed his scotch, then detached himself from the group of men and made his way toward me, extending his hand like a prince in a fairy tale.

"You look absolutely stunning," he said.

The gleam in his eye made me believe him, and I let myself relax. Well, as much as I could knowing he could flip the switch at any moment and have me struggling for control.

"Thank you, Mr. Drake. I've never worn anything like this… I…"

"Shh," he said, sensing where I was going. "If you're to be mine, you must let me treat you, Isabeau." He leaned in to whisper in my ear, placing his hand at the small of my back. "You picked my favorite. I can't wait to tear it off you later."

I quivered beneath his touch, my breath hitching at the thought of being taken by this man again, of being his tonight.

"Come now. I have people I want to introduce you to."

He led me through the crowd, the heat from his hand distracting, to say the least. What I wouldn't give for it to slip lower, and all these people to disappear, leaving us alone together. As we approached a group mingling by floor-to-ceiling glass windows, the egg buzzed to life again, making me whimper.

Mr. Drake gave me a sideways grin. *He's enjoying this far too much.* I pursed my lips and glared back, letting him know he wouldn't break me. I steadied my steps despite the pulsing making my stomach tighten and my thighs tremble. *Keep it together, Isabeau!*

"Were your ears burning, Chase? We were just talking about you! Who is this lovely creature on your arm?"

A middle aged woman with sleek black hair smiled at me. I suppressed a shudder as the egg began pulsing harder. Mr. Drake's hand was in his pocket—a bemused half smile on his handsome face. That bastard.

"Allow me to introduce Isabeau Willcox, my date tonight. Isabeau, this is Maria Coldwell, president of the Chamber of Commerce."

My mouth fell open, and I struggled to think. *Buzz Buzz Buzz* filled my head, even as it filled my body, making me tense again and again.

I held out a shaking hand. "It's a pleasure… uhh… to meet you, Madam President."

The buzzing ceased, and I sucked in a sharp breath, then

smiled, trying to cover for my odd behavior.

"Maria will be just fine. This is a party, after all," she said, beaming. "You watch out for this one, Isabeau. He's a real lady killer."

She barked a laugh and gave Mr. Drake a playful shove. For the briefest of moments, I thought I saw him blush, but then the egg buzzed between my legs again, and my mind went blank. Everything I had in me was focused on not giving in to the sensation and dropping to my knees, arching my back as I came, howling like an animal.

I tried to tamp down the pleasure bubbling up inside me, but Mr. Drake was making it pulse over and over again, torturing me as I stood beside him.

"Isabeau," he said, guiding me toward an attractive man in his thirties. "Please meet my partner, Alexander Smith."

The pulsing continued, and I suppressed a groan. *Buzz Buzz.Buzz.*

"Pleased to meet you, Mr. Smith," I said between gritted teeth.

Buzzzzzzz.

Alexander Smith grinned, looking almost wolfish for a moment, his black eyes full of mischief.

"Chase has told me so much about you, Isabeau, but none of it did you justice."

He's very handsome. And young, like Mr. Drake. I wonder what he heard about me?

The thoughts came unbidden. My mind was a mess as I tried desperately to maintain control, even as my orgasm threatened to unravel me right here and now. I shifted, digging the point of my high heel into the arch of my other foot. The pain soothed me, bringing me back down.

For a moment. *Buzz. Buzz. Buzzzzzz.*

He took my hand in his and kissed it gently, the feel of his lips on my skin adding to the pressure building inside me.

Mr. Drake stepped between Alexander and I, suddenly looking flustered. The buzzing stopped abruptly.

"That's enough, *Lex*. She's not here to be drooled on."

"Except by you, you mean," he said, smiling in a way that made me uncomfortable. "Please to meet you, Isabeau."

He winked at me and made his way back through the crowd.

Mr. Drake's hand was on the small of my back again, leading me toward the bar, away from Mr. Smith.

"So that was your partner? The Smith of Drake & Smith?"

"Indeed."

He handed me a glass of white wine, and I sipped it gratefully.

"I never see him in the offices," I said.

"He prefers to work in the field, traveling the globe... seducing client's daughters," he said, his voice suddenly dark.

"I see you don't care for him much."

Mr. Drake ran his hand over my bare back, stroking it in a way that made my core clench again, squeezing the egg. I shivered.

"You see a lot."

The pulsing began again, and I smiled up at him, shaking my head. "You are a very bad man."

He signaled the staff, and instantly music began playing. I pressed my thighs together, trying to keep control as couples began moving to the middle of the foyer and dancing, gliding across the marble floor.

Without asking, Mr. Drake led me into the crowd, gathering me firmly in his arms. My breath caught in my chest being this close to him, and my eyes watered as I neared the peak, trying desperately to scramble back from the edge.

He leaned close, his nose brushing my cheek. "Cum for me, Isabeau."

And just like that, I came, my pleasure bursting forth, running over like a river flooding its bank. I stiffened in his arms and moaned softly in his ear, shaking gently against him as he steered me on the dance floor. I could feel his erection pressing against my belly; his need for me as evident as mine was for him.

I was panting, my lace underwear now soaking wet. The buzzing stopped, but I kept trembling in his arms, aftershocks of my orgasm still ripping through me. I looked around, hoping no one would notice my flushed face, or my shaking limbs. Had anyone seen?

"You're so beautiful when you cum," Mr. Drake said, his voice low and heated. "You are so responsive… so obedient."

I sighed at his words, my heart pounding in my chest. "I… I wanted to please you."

His hand tightened on my back, pulling me harder against him. "I wish I could fuck you right here. Right now…" He made a frustrated noise like a grunt. "This party is over."

He reached between us, adjusting himself, then led me to the foot of the staircase, where he stood side by side with me. He signaled to Mr. Daniels and the music ceased immediately. There was a murmur from the crowd, then all eyes and ears were on Mr. Drake, and, to my embarrassment, me.

"Ladies and gentleman, I'm sorry to have to announce this, but I find I'm not feeling very well. I'm afraid I'm going to have to cut this party short."

There was a general "ohh" of regret from the patrons, before people began moving for their purses and stoles.

"Thank you all so much for coming. I hope to see you all again soon. Drive safely!"

He beamed out over the crowd, bowing slightly toward Maria and her party. The guests began shuffling out under the keen eye of Mr. Daniels. Mr. Drake took my hand and led me upstairs without another word, not bothering to see if any guests had complaints or that everyone made it out of his home. Apparently, he had people for that.

My head spun thinking about the nonchalant way he just dismissed all of those people from his party. And how quickly they obeyed him.

We rounded the corner, but I didn't make it two steps before he slammed me against the wall.

"I want you," he growled. "Now."

His hands were under my dress, then, gripping my ass, kneading my flesh. I moaned, writhing in his grasp, pushing myself against his hardness, now rubbing against me through his suit.

"Yes," I breathed. I wanted him so badly it hurt, my body aching for him.

His lips met mine, his mouth bruising me as he kissed me roughly, his tongue forcing its way into my mouth. I groaned into him, my tongue tasting his, teasing, wanting to be closer to him as quickly as possible.

He broke away, leaving me breathless. "Not here."

I squealed as he bent down and threw me over his shoulder, then jogged down the hall toward his study. My skirt was hitched too high up, my ass feeling the breeze as he moved. I hoped to God there were no staff members up here who would see this undignified display, but even if they did, the embarrassment was worth it for him. For what would come next. For what I'd longed for all day long while I thought of him.

He threw open the door to the study, then slammed it behind him and pushed the mechanism by the fireplace that opened the entrance to his dungeon. Once inside, he snapped it shut, leaving us blissfully alone.

"Take the egg out," he commanded.

We were both breathing hard, his eyes glinting with the same need I felt. With my eyes locked on his, I reached between my legs and eased my panties down over my heels. He held out his hand, and I placed them in it, gasping as he brought them to his nose and inhaled.

"God, yes, Isabeau. You smell amazing."

I reached carefully between my legs and squeezed my muscles, easing the toy out of my body. He snatched it away, breathing that in as well before setting it aside on one of the dark, wooden shelves.

"You're ready for me." It wasn't a question.

"Yes, Sir."

He grinned wickedly. "Then hold up your arms and brace yourself."

I smiled, then bit my lip, arousal and fear rushing through me, intermingling into sweet anticipation. He shed his jacket and shirt, then advanced upon me, pushing me back against the wall beneath a metal grating over head. He grabbed the bottom of my dress and ripped it off over my head, tearing the silk up the side. I made a noise in protest—it was so expensive!—but he glared at me until I shut my mouth, holding my hands still above my head.

He slung a chain up over the grating, then down again, and I noticed two leather cuffs dangling overhead.

"Wrap your legs around my waist," he said, picking me up.

I did as I was told, wrapping my naked legs around him, letting him support me as he cuffed first my left wrist, then the right. I was hanging then, at just the right height for him to take me, but too high for my feet to touch the ground on my own. I mewled, feeling helpless and trapped, and totally turned on.

He leaned back, letting me slip just a little, and I shrieked as I thought he was going to let me fall. My weight settled on the cuffs, and I gripped the chain, holding on tight.

"What's the matter, little slave? Don't you trust me?"

He reached down, unzipping himself. "Hang on for me."

He let me go, and I dangled, then, unsupported and afraid, trying not to scream, feeling like a true slave succumbing to his will. There was nothing I could do. I watched him roll a condom on, and then he was back, wrapping my legs around him, supporting me before my arms could get too sore.

"I'm glad you changed your mind," he growled, and thrust himself inside of me, impaling me on his girth.

I cried out, my body overly sensitive from the orgasm he'd already given me, every nerve on fire as he filled me the way I so desperately needed. He pulled all the way out, and dipped a finger into my wetness, then thrust back inside.

I moaned, loving the way he fit just right, stretching me to an almost painful degree. His fingers dug into my ass cheeks as he began moving, stroking in and out of me as I held onto the chain for dear life. When his finger found my pucker, I gasped against him.

"I love this ass of yours, little slave. The things I'm going to do to you here," he growled, fucking me harder.

I yelled as the tip of his finger pushed past the ring of muscle, stinging and sending jolts of pleasure through me simultaneously as he invaded me.

"Would you like that, slave? Would you like to be taken in the ass by your master?"

He gripped my waist with his other hand, pulling me up and down onto his cock harder than ever, bucking up into me with each thrust, his finger working its way further into my ass as he spoke.

"Y-yes!" I cried.

I'd never had a man there before, but the way he said what he wanted to do to me made me weak with desire. I wanted him to take me everywhere. I wanted to be totally his and learn at his hand.

"Good girl," he grunted.

He removed his finger, then roughly pulled my bra down over my breasts, trussing them up before him. He held me in both arms now, and leaned in, suckling first one nipple into his mouth, then the other as he pumped in and out of my eager body. I wanted to run my fingers through his hair, to caress him and hold him, but I was his prisoner, trapped above, being used for his will, and his alone.

I screamed as he bit a nipple and slapped my ass hard. The stinging made my pussy clench around him, ratcheting up my pleasure in a way that made my head spin. He moved to the other nipple and bit down, spanking me again, and again as he made me his, taking me harder and faster.

My arms were growing tired, and I could no longer hold the chain for support. I hung there, trusting him as he slapped and bit and slid in and out of me, covering my body in a riot of sensation, pain and pleasure merging into one beautiful symphony of desire.

He licked his way up to my neck, teasing and kissing, even as he mercilessly fucked me from below. I was wailing now, my voice echoing off the walls as I rode him. When his teeth closed on my throat, I came undone, my orgasm crashing over me, my heartbeat thudding in my ears as he bit me harder, marking me.

His hands clenched my ass hard, and he moaned against my skin. His erection jumped inside of me, and I knew he was cumming, filling me with his hot seed. For a moment, I wished we didn't have the condom between us, but the thought flickered away as another convulsion took me, making my eyes roll back in my head.

His bites turned to kisses as he held me close, thrusting in one last, slow time before finally pulling out. He crushed me to him as he undid my restraints, then lowered my feet gently to the floor. My legs felt like they might fail, and I leaned against him, smiling and exhausted.

"Oh, Isa," he said, and kissed my hair. "Please tell me you'll be mine. Tell me you really have changed your mind?"

I nodded, and pulled back so I could look into his eyes. "I trust you, Sir… I'll be yours."

He swept me into his arms, kissing me tenderly in a way that made my toes curl all over again. When he broke away and moved toward the shelves, I knew what was coming next. He brought me the box containing the two collars and opened it, offering it to me once again.

I reached in and took the leather one, rolling it over in my fingers. It was soft, but strong. *Just like me*, I thought, and smiled at the notion. He helped me buckle it on, then led me to a mirror on one side of the room. We stood side by side, him with his suit pants still on, me with my breasts bursting out of my bra, and his collar around my neck. I ran my fingers over it, admiring the way it looked. The way it fit.

The way it made me feel.

"I'm really yours," I said softly, and he nodded beside

me.

"Isabeau, you have no idea what kind of things I have in store for you. We'll begin your training tomorrow, in the office."

"My training?" My eyes widened, but I had to admit, I liked the sound of that.

He ran his fingers over the tops of my breasts, his green eyes boring into mine, even in our reflection.

"Oh yes. Every submissive needs training. How else will you know how to please me?"

I shivered beneath that stare. *Training at his hand*... and in the office, no less!

"I think I'm going to enjoy this," I said.

Mr. Drake slapped my ass, and grinned in the dim light of the dungeon. "I'll make sure of that, little slave."

5 AT HIS INSTRUCTION

That night, I finally shared a bed with the mysterious Mr. Drake.

He slid a silk robe over my shoulders, and led me from his dungeon, through the study, and up yet another flight of stairs to the top level of the mansion—the floor I'd never set foot on, afraid I'd be trespassing.

He led me down a hallway with no other doors until we reached the end. There was nothing but an intricately carved black door with no knob. Mr. Drake reached into his pocket and removed a tarnished silver key, then fit it into a lock that blended almost perfectly with the scrollwork.

More secrets, I thought with a smile. *My, but he is mysterious.* But perhaps when you were as rich as Mr. Drake was, you were allowed a few eccentricities. I certainly wasn't complaining.

He smirked at me as the key turned, his eyes glinting in the darkness.

"I've never invited a woman into this bedroom before," he said.

I raised an eyebrow. "Never?"

He ran a hand slowly down my spine, stroking me in a way that made me shiver beneath the robe.

"I usually send my lovers home, or they sleep in a

separate room. You're the first, Isa… What do you do to me?" He turned the knob, and pushed inward. Low lights came on, illuminating the room. "You're different from all the rest."

I wanted to believe that, but, unbidden, a small voice inside my head whispered *What's so special about you?* A pit formed in my stomach, but I tried to tamp it down; to focus only on him and this moment. Now was not the time to worry about if, or when, he'd tire of me and move on. I was here to enjoy myself… for as long as it lasted.

"You're not so bad yourself," I said, smiling up at him.

He took my hand and led me into his room. I looked around and gasped. Floor-to-ceiling windows replaced the three walls I'd been expecting, the entire room surrounded by glass except for the wall behind us. Stars twinkled outside, making the black, four-poster bed look like it was perched on a cliff at the edge of the world.

"The glass is treated, so no one can see in. Do you like the view?"

I felt almost dizzy standing there, with the giant windows broken up only by black columns in the corners of the master bedroom. The floor was hardwood with a thick, crimson rug covering it, giving the room a decadent feel. Deep red sheets covered the bed, contrasting sharply with the dark wood.

The corner of my mouth turned up in a smile. The room was so sensual and dramatic. It was so *him*.

"I love it."

He came over to me and released the tie of my robe. The silk slithered to the floor.

"We can be as naked as the day we were born in here, and no one will be the wiser."

His hand closed around my throat, his thumb caressing my skin in a way that raised the hairs on my arm and made my pussy clench. I was still deliciously sore from our lovemaking, but even so, I wanted more.

"I can fuck you here, take you any way I want you, and no one will see, while we stare out over the city… Would you like that, Isabeau?"

My breathing became ragged, and I could see his pupils darkening as he spoke.

"Yes, Sir," I whispered.

The air between us was electric. His green eyes bored into mine, and he slipped his boxers off slowly. I licked my lips as his erection sprang free. I couldn't believe he was already hard again, ready for me once more.

In a flash, his hands were one me, forcing me around and making me stumble toward the nearest wall.

"Bend over," he growled, "and put your palms against the glass."

I did as he asked, leaning slowly toward the window, but as I looked down, it felt like I was dangling over the edge of the three-story building, the city lights twinkling below us from our vantage point on the hill. A car passed, its headlights illuminating the street, the concrete a reminder of what waited for me if the glass shattered. I swallowed hard and hesitated, a spike of fear rushing through me.

I'd never been afraid of heights, but this was something else altogether.

A hand came down on my backside, making me yelp in pain.

"Bend *over*. It's perfectly safe."

"Yes, Sir."

I placed shaking hands on the window and leaned my weight against it, my breath catching in my chest, a rush of adrenaline making my pulse hammer. I heard the rip of a condom wrapper behind me, then felt his rough hands kneading my ass.

"You're so beautiful like this, Isa. Bent over, ready and waiting for me to do as I please..."

I felt his fingers between my legs, caressing my sex, and moaned, my breath fogging the glass.

"So wet for me..."

He dipped one finger inside of me, and I squeezed around him, loving the way he felt inside me. Then, it was gone, and I heard a soft sucking noise behind me.

"And you taste so sweet."

My body responded to his words, my arousal leaking onto my thighs. I couldn't believe this man—how sensual and raw he was—and most of all, that he wanted me the way that he did. The same way I wanted him.

He gripped my hips hard, his fingers bruising me. I felt the tip of his cock spreading me open, and groaned, needy and desperate to be filled. With a grunt, he sheathed himself inside of me in one hard stroke, pushing me up against the glass.

My head spun, looking down from such a height, but his arm around my waist held me steady, making me feel safe even as he pulled out slowly, then thrust again, hard.

"You feel so goddamn good, Isa," he growled in my ear.

He reached around and found my nipples, pulling and teasing, making me gasp as he pinched one, then the other, sending sharp, delicious pain coursing through me. My thighs squeezed together, tightening around him as he entered me again and again, pounding harder as he held me pinned beneath him.

I could smell his sweat mingling with the musky smell of sex clinging to the both of us, and beneath that a unique and heavenly note that was all *him*. Chase Drake.

He yanked me back onto him roughly, making me cry out as he hit me deeper with each stroke of his cock. When he reached between my legs and pinched my clit, I screamed, my orgasm crashing over me before I knew what was happening, my legs trembling with the force of my convulsions.

"Yes, Isa," he groaned. "God, yes... Milk me with your pussy."

He didn't let up, his fingers pulling on my sensitive nub as I spasmed around him, my eyes rolling up toward the stars, drinking in the night sky even as I felt stars bursting inside of me. With another pump, he drew out oh-so-slowly before slamming home one last time. He cried my name as he spent himself inside of me, and in that moment, I felt alive in a way I never had before.

In that moment, I was happy.

Afterward, he carried me to his bed, threw back the covers and draped my exhausted body on top of the soft sheets. He crawled in next to me and held me close, putting my head on his shoulder, his arms holding me tight to his chest. He kissed my hair, and I fell asleep, smiling into the darkness.

***

I awoke to an empty bed, a pile of new, designer clothing I'd never seen before, and a note.

Of course.

I rolled my eyes, wondering what Mr. Drake had written this time. We were supposed to go to work today, after all. *But he said he would train you,* a little voice inside me whispered. *In the office, no less!*

I had to leave early to prepare some things at the office. Please help yourself to breakfast and dress in the clothing I laid out for you. A car is waiting to bring you to work.

I raised an eyebrow, then picked up the skirt neatly folded at the end of the bed. The quality was impeccable. The label caught my eye, and I swallowed hard. *Gucci?* How could I accept this? But then again, I only had my clothes from yesterday, wrinkled up and God-knows-where. Maybe I could wear the clothes he bought today, and return them later?

I shook my head. Who knew it would be so stressful sleeping with a billionaire? I looked back at the note, the last line turning my frown back into a smile.

I can't wait to see you, Isa.

My whole body tingled with anticipation at the thought of seeing my Mr. Drake, gorgeous and put together in his expensive suit. *I can't wait either, Sir.*

Grinning like a schoolgirl with a crush, I began to get ready. After all, it was a work day. I had to look professional.

***

As the elevator doors slid open, I took a deep breath, preparing myself for the day ahead. I knew I had transcriptions waiting for me, but beyond that, I had no idea what Mr. Drake had in mind. Would he put me to work, as usual, or would he put me flat on my back?

I grinned at the thought.

My new heels clicked on the marble as I approached my desk. A package sat on my chair, smartly wrapped in silver paper. There was a post-it on top, with instructions written in sharpie.

Come to my office immediately. Bring the box.

I exhaled sharply. *Well, then. I suppose I should get in there. Boss' orders.*

But instead of rushing to him, I took my time, setting the box next to me as I logged in to my computer, punched in for the day, then checked my inbox for urgent items. I suppressed a smile, wondering if he was watching me through that camera of his, going slowly crazy waiting for me to come to him.

I placed my purse into my drawer and locked it before finally getting to my feet. I smoothed down the new skirt, feeling strong and capable in my low cut silk blouse, instead of out of place, as I'd feared. Perhaps the clothes do make the woman? Or maybe I was simply adjusting to living at the edge of Mr. Drake's world.

I rapped on the door.

"About time, Miss Willcox."

So he was *watching*. My lips twitched as I pushed the door open.

Mr. Drake was sitting at the edge of his desk, waiting, his body tense, like a snake coiled and ready to strike.

"What took you so long?"

His eyes were intense, but I thought I saw a trace of humor behind them, even though his face was impassive.

"I came as soon as I could, Mr. Drake. After doing my due-diligence for my position, that is."

He stroked his chin, eying me from head to toe. A moment passed, and I wondered if he was going to punish me. The thought made my pussy heat.

"Very well, Isabeau. You're nothing if not thorough. Now, please. Come here, and open that box. I think you'll like what's inside."

I undid the paper carefully, then folded it and set it on his desk. I noticed the approval in his eyes when I looked up. *I knew he'd like that.* Somehow it just didn't feel right to rip wrapping paper in front of Mr. Drake. It was sloppy. And he doesn't tolerate sloppiness.

I raised the lid of the box and my mouth fell open. Inside were two long, black leather gloves, covered in laces and buckles. I didn't know what to make of them. I lifted one out, my skin humming at the feel of the supple material.

"What are these for?"

Mr. Drake's eyes burned into mine. "They are bondage opera gloves, little temp. With them, I can restrain you in a myriad of ways. But today, I'll use them to keep your arms bound behind your back."

I looked back down at the glove in my hand, tracing the metal eyelets and laces with my fingertip. The thought of being bound by him made my body come alive. I licked my lips.

"Oh."

"I told you your training would begin today, Isa. Are you

still my willing slave?"

He ran a hand over my face, and I trembled at his touch. It felt like time stopped for a moment, and as I looked at him, I knew I wanted this more than anything. To be his. To please him. *To let him please me*, the little voice inside me said, and I smiled, knowing I was ready for whatever he had to give me.

"Yes, Sir."

His hand knotted in my hair, and he pulled me close. The twinge of pain made me even hotter. A soft moan escaped my lips as he brought his face just inches from mine.

"You're going to learn how to perform on your knees today, slave. I'm going to feed you my cock, inch by inch, until you learn how to take it all. Would you like that?"

He yanked my hair, tilting my head up and making me gasp.

"Yes… Sir."

I'd been fantasizing about tasting him for days now, wondering what he would feel like stretching my lips, what he would taste like on my tongue.

His lips met mine, hot and urgent, and I opened to him, moaning into his mouth. When we broke apart, his breathing was ragged, his pupils dark and dangerous.

"On. Your. Knees."

I did as he asked, dropping to my knees, my brain buzzing with anticipation. I noticed with a grin that the skirt he bought me had hidden side slits that made the position easy. *Nice touch.*

"When you come to me in here, I expect you on your knees, ready for my commands. Is that understood?"

I nodded, my own breathing harsh. "Yes, Sir."

I felt myself getting wet for him, my body eager to be used.

"Now, spread your legs apart, Isa, and put your hands behind your back."

I spread my knees wider, sitting back on my heels. I felt wanton and vulnerable like this, open and waiting. Perhaps it was wrong to like that feeling of vulnerability, but something about trusting him like this was so erotic, it banished all thoughts of propriety, my former ideas about sex forgotten.

He moved behind me and knelt down, slowly undoing the buttons of my blouse before untucking it from my skirt and sliding it off my shoulders. The cool air from the office hit my breasts, shielded only by my thin, lace bra, and my nipples tightened against the fabric.

"Hold your arms out behind you, slave."

I stretched my arms out behind my back, and sighed as I felt him tug the cool leather up over my skin. He moved slowly, sensually, tugging first one opera glove on, then the other, before running his fingers between mine, making sure the fit was tight.

"I'm going to lace you up now. You won't be able to move until I release you. Understood?"

I nodded, adrenaline coursing through me at the thought of being restrained like this. I felt the laces tug, the gloves tightening together, drawing my arms inward until they were pressed together behind my spine. It was a stretch, the feeling at once frightening and arousing. He jerked the buckles closed above the laces, the leather biting into my skin at the top of my arms, then securing my elbows and wrists, making sure I was held firmly in place.

I wasn't going anywhere.

My breasts jutted out as my shoulder blades pressed toward one another. I felt so deliciously naughty, spread open for him on his office floor, ready to be taken any way he wanted me.

His hands were in my hair again, tilting my head to one side.

"You are absolutely stunning," he said, his breath tickling my neck.

He ran his tongue over my skin, tasting me. "Are you ready to begin your training?"

"Oh, yes," I said, closing my eyes as his lips grazed my ear.

His hand jerked my hair, making me yelp in surprise.

"Yes, what?"

"Yes, Sir!" My panties were soaking wet now, and I wondered if he could smell how turned on I was.

"Good girl."

He stood up and crossed in front of me. His hands went to his fly, and he undid his zipper, the fabric of his flat front suit parting tantalizing slowly. He reached in, drawing out his rock hard erection, and I opened my mouth, ready and eager to taste him.

"Run your tongue over the tip," he said.

He leaned toward me, bringing the head of his beautiful cock to my lips. I leaned forward and licked the slit, moaning as the salty taste of his pre-cum slid over my taste buds. He smelled like expensive soap and that musky scent that was all his own. I inhaled, letting him fill my senses, then ran my tongue in fat strokes over the entire glans.

His breath hissed between his teeth, his rod giving a little jump against my mouth.

"Yes, Isa... very good."

He groaned as I went back for more, lapping and nibbling at the tender spot just beneath the head.

"Now, take me inside. Wrap your lips around me. Slowly now..."

He didn't have to tell me twice. I opened wide, wanting, needing more of him. True to his word, he guided himself into my mouth, patiently feeding his cock to me. I ran my tongue over the ridge on the underside as I swallowed him, groaning around his length. I loved the taste of him, the feeling of being filled in this new way. I'd given boyfriends oral before, but never had it been this slow, this sensual. Never had I wanted to please them so badly, my own sex throbbing with each flick of my tongue.

I sucked harder as he urged more of himself into my wet mouth.

"Oh, God, Isa. You're far too good at this."

He wrapped his hands in my hair and drew himself out,

all the way to the tip, before slowly pumping back in. I lapped at him as he did, smiling around him as I watching his eyes close above me and his body twitch.

Suddenly, even though I was the one on my knees, I felt powerful, controlling him like this. I was making him feel this, here and now, turning him on as much as he was me. I suckled harder, bobbing my head over him even as he began slowly fucking my face. I moaned again, the vibrations making him clench his jaw above me.

"You keep this up, and I'm going to cum, little temp," he said through gritted teeth.

He pulled out of my mouth with a wet pop. "Not yet."

I frowned and leaned forward, trying to recapture him with my mouth.

His hand came down, slapping my breast.

"What do you think you're doing, slave? I said not yet! You are such an eager thing, aren't you?"

"Yes, I am, Sir," I said, looking up at him defiantly.

I wanted him. If I could have moved my arms, I would have stroked that gorgeous dick of his, cupping his balls until he came then and there, but I was trapped. Helpless to do as I pleased. Waiting on his instruction.

He looked down at me, appraising me with a bemused expression on his face.

"What am I to do with you?"

I could feel the burning heat inside of me, begging for release. Not only his, but mine. I was so aroused, I ached.

His hand closed lightly around my throat again.

"Stand up, Isa."

He pulled upward, and I gasped, before pushing myself onto my feet. His hand steadied me, then pulled me close.

"You want me now? Then I'll fuck you blue until you cum, little slave. But later, you're going to kneel beneath me, and get exactly what you deserve for being such a bad girl."

"Oh God," I breathed.

The little voice inside me screamed *Yes, Yes, YES!*

He pulled me to him, kissing me hard, his hands roughly

squeezing my breasts through the lace. He pinched my nipples, twisting sharply with both hands. I cried out, tears stinging the corners of my eyes, my sex tingling at the jolt of pain.

"Trust me, Isa."

With that, he spun me around and bent me over, holding me by the leather gloves tying my arms together. I screeched, fear stabbing through me as I hung in his grasp, feeling like I was falling, even as he held me fast.

His weight shifted as one hand let go, and I pressed my lips together, trying not to scream, willing myself to trust my master, my Mr. Drake. There was a tearing noise, like foil meeting teeth, then rustling behind me.

I breathed deeply, trying to relax, hanging doubled over by my wrists like I was. Then, my skirt was yanked up over my ass, my panties ripped at the crotch, and he was there, pressing into me, his cock driving into my channel without hesitation.

I moaned, clenching around him, my body already thrumming with excitement. His other hand held me now, and he jerked me back, slamming into me as his hips met mine. His balls slapped forward with each stroke, hitting my sensitive folds. I cried out again and again as he thrust deep inside, my pussy aching from the pounding, my pleasure spiraling upward with each violent thrust.

He jerked me upward, wrapping his arm around my waist as he continued fucking me, harder and harder, faster and faster, our bodies making slapping sounds that echoed through the office. His teeth sunk into my shoulder, making me groan, but when he pinched my clit, I screamed as I came, my pussy convulsing around him, squeezing him for all I was worth.

He grunted behind me, pinching my bud again and again, making tears flow down my cheeks even as I soared on the wings of my orgasm, my whole body shaking in his arms. Then he held me tight, pressing me against him as he came, his seed hot inside of me, his erection twitching even as my muscles tightened around him, milking every last drop.

"Fuck," he said, and kissed my neck softly. "You are something else, little temp. How do you do this to me every time?"

I leaned back against him, feeling weak, my legs threatening to give out.

"I could ask you the same thing. Sir."

I felt him smiling against my shoulder.

"We have to clean up now. I have a meeting in 45 minutes. A meeting you'll be attending."

"Yes, Sir. I'm happy to serve."

And I meant it.

***

"*What?*"

"You heard me perfectly well, Isa. Do I have to bend you over my knee, or will you obey?"

The thought of a good spanking didn't sound much like a punishment, but I refused to be distracted.

"You want me to suck you off under your desk while you take your meeting?" I imagined it, my nipples hardening beneath my bra. "Won't we get caught?"

He grinned at me, tenting his fingers behind his desk. "Not if you're quiet, as I instructed."

I stared at him, at this powerful, apparently *crazy* man, who wanted to live out this sexual fantasy on company time. He ran a hand through his wavy hair, his eyes shining, full of excitement. I had to admit… the thought of doing something so damn wrong made me horny as hell.

Who was I turning into? This wasn't like responsible old Isabeau, who always did things by the book; dependable Isabeau who always had a cool head and kept things under control. That girl didn't do things like this. Not by a long shot.

But she also didn't have a whole lot of fun, I thought. My sex throbbed deliciously in agreement.

"If you're going to do this, we need to get ready. The meeting starts in ten minutes. If not, I'll understand, but it will mean the end of our training today."

His smile was gone, and he watched me with trepidation. *Oh, what the hell.*

The old Isabeau would never have put her heart on the line to be with a man like this, either. Would never have dared to think she was worthy. Would never have trusted him when he said he wanted her to be his… Fuck the old Isabeau. In with the new!

"I'm ready, Sir."

His face lit up, and a wave of affection surged through me. If I could make him smile like that, any risk was worth it.

"Then, lets get you out of those clothes, slave. I want you naked, handcuffed, and hungry for my cock."

Oh, dear Lord. His words made my pussy tingle beneath my skirt. I pressed my thighs together, trying not to squirm under that gaze.

"Yes, Sir," I whispered, and undid the clasp of my bra.

***

When the knock came on the door, I was crouched beneath the large, mahogany desk, shielded from view by the wooden front piece that went all the way down to the floor. My hands were secured behind my back with soft leather cuffs, and I was naked from head to toe, my hair pulled back in a braid to keep it out of my face.

I tingled from my scalp all the way down to my toes in anticipation. Mr. Drake adjusted himself in his leather chair, unzipping his pants and freeing his hard on. It looked good enough to eat, and I leaned forward, eager to get started.

"Come in."

The sounds of the door whispering open then clicking shut reached my ears as I leaned forward and wrapped my lips around his length. I wanted to groan around him, but I did as I was told and kept silent, smirking to myself at the thought of what I was doing. It was just. So. Wrong.

And so deliciously exciting.

"How are you, Chase? Having a good day?"

I heard the creak of leather as the man sat down across from Mr. Drake. I laved the bottom of his erection slowly so I wouldn't make any slurping noises. His cock gave a little jump in my mouth, and I glowed inside, knowing how much he was loving this from his body's reaction.

"You have no idea. You?"

"Good, good. But we didn't come here to exchange pleasantries, did we?"

There was something very familiar about that voice. It had a sarcastic edge to it that I remembered from... somewhere. I relaxed my throat and leaned down, taking as much of him as I could into my mouth. Mr. Drake's thigh tensed against the side of my face.

"Fair enough, Lex. What have you got for me?"

Lex. The business partner. I wondered what he'd think of Mr. Drake if he knew what was happening right under his nose. My pussy leaked onto my thigh at the thought of him, just a couple of feet away, oblivious to the naked woman sucking cock beneath the desk.

There was a slap as a stack of paper fell onto the desk.

"Our projections look like they were wrong, Chase. Earnings were down, but not enough to worry about yet. It's probably just the economy catching up to us."

"How much... how much are we talking about?"

I suppressed a giggle under the desk. I'd just sucked one of his balls into my mouth, rolling my tongue over it before moving to the other, making him skip a beat. I was impressed that Mr. Drake was keeping it together so well. It felt like sweet revenge for making me wear that vibrator to his party. I never thought torturing him would feel so good. He did ask for it, after all.

"Like I said. It's nothing to worry about. Here are the

figures if you'd like to look through them later. We're just down a percentage or two instead of the growth we'd hoped for."

Mr. Drake grunted, either in displeasure at the news, or because I'd just taken his length all the way into my mouth again, and was busy quietly pumping up and down, running my tongue over the bottom ridge the whole way.

His hand reached down and grabbed my braid, holding me onto him. The tip of his cock hit the back of my throat, and I breathed through my nose, willing myself not to gag. He tensed, and then he was cumming, his saltiness filling my mouth. I suppressed a groan and swallowed greedily, drinking him in.

"Thank you for gathering those numbers, Lex. If I have any questions, I'll give you a call."

Boy, was he smooth. He was cool as a cucumber, even after what felt to me like an intense orgasm.

There was a sharp rap at the door, then the sound of it swinging open before Mr. Drake could say 'come in.'

"There you are, Chasey," a female voice cooed. "Your secretary wasn't out there, so I just let myself in. I hope I'm not interrupting."

Chasey? I sat back, releasing Mr. Drake from between my lips, and listened hard.

"Veronica? What the hell are you doing here?"

The coldness of Mr. Drake's tone made me relax a little. I just hoped he wouldn't have to go anywhere, considering what we'd just been doing.

"Now, now, Chase," Lex teased. "Is that any way to talk to the future Mrs. Drake?"

I sat up with a start, bumping my head on the bottom of the desk. I winced silently. *Did he just say what I thought he said?* A feminine giggle masked the sound, making the hair on my neck stand on end. Suddenly, the cuffs on my wrists chafed, and I wished I were anywhere but here.

"It's okay. You know how he gets. He's just a cranky puss, aren't you Chasey?"

If I had to listen to this for too much longer, I was in danger of puking on Mr. Drake's shoes. Who was this woman?

"Please, Veronica. Now isn't a good time."

His tone was dark. Forceful. But from the sound of her grating laugh, it had no effect on this *Veronica*.

"It's never a good time! I'm not leaving until you agree to join me for dinner at your parents' house tonight. They invited us, but said you haven't returned any of their calls, you naughty thing."

I wanted to growl in frustration, trapped like a naked rat under his desk. I shouldn't be here. I shouldn't be hearing these things.

An exasperated sigh met my ears.

"I have some things to wrap up here, Veronica, and then can meet you downstairs. We'll discuss it there. Lex, if you'll please escort her to the lobby?"

There was the sound of shuffling paper, and Mr. Drake tapping a pen on the desk impatiently.

"Always a pleasure Chase," Lex said.

There was the sound of a huffy female sigh, then footsteps. The door clicked shut and silence filled the office. Mr. Drake waited for a few moments before tucking himself back into his pants and sliding his chair back.

"Isa... It's not what it sounds like."

Humiliation coursing through me, I clambered out from under the desk and turned around, holding my wrists out.

"Let me go."

He worked the buckle on one cuff, rubbing my wrist. Tears stung my eyes. I wanted to pull away. I wanted to gather my clothing and leave and never speak to him again. But when he rubbed my wrist that way, part of me wanted to stay, to believe that things weren't how they seemed.

But then who was that woman? And why had Lex called her "the future Mrs. Drake?"

He released the other cuff. "Isa, she's a friend of the family."

I turned around, my eyes on the floor, avoiding his. "I see."

She's rich. She's one of them. I reached for the drawer where he'd stashed my clothing, and a tear rolled down my cheek, despite my best efforts to hold it in. *I'm just a secretary in borrowed clothing. How can I compete with that?*

Mr. Drake touched my shoulder as I jammed my legs into the skirt and zipped it up.

"I want you. No one else."

"Then you're not going to dinner with her?"

I buttoned the blouse, my fingers shaking as I worked.

"I… I have to go."

I slid on my heels and grabbed my purse, spilling chapstick and receipts onto the floor. "Then, so do I."

And before he could say anything else, I walked out of the office and slammed the door, leaving Chase Drake stunned and silent. I stabbed at the elevator button, the light blurring through the tears now flowing freely down my cheeks.

I expected the office door to open and for him to come after me. To tell me again that I was the one, not her. I waited to hear him call my name.

The bell chimed, and the elevator slid open. I took a deep breath, and stepped inside.

6 AT HIS WORD

The elevator doors slid shut, and I gasped for air as hot tears rolled down my cheeks. The car shuddered as it started moving, and for a moment, I felt like the floor dropped out from underneath me, that everything was slipping away. And maybe it was.

I took a deep breath and wiped my face as the elevator slowed to a stop. Someone from the next floor down was getting on, and I didn't want a stranger to see me crying. I worked here, after all. It would be no good for the whole company to know that Mr. Drake's new assistant was weeping in the elevator.

The doors slid open, and I shuffled back to make room, my eyes downcast. The doors slid shut, but instead of pushing the button for the floor he wanted, the man who entered slammed his hand onto the red "stop" button.

"Don't run from me like that again," Mr. Drake said.

My eyes snapped upward, meeting his. His hair was disheveled, his breathing catching up like he'd run down a flight of stairs. And I suppose he had.

"You came after me."

I was in shock, standing there, staring at my boss, my eyes still full of tears threatening to spill over once again. He took two steps and pinned me against the mirrored wall of the elevator, his hands on either side of me, effectively trapping me.

"You didn't let me explain."

I looked down at my shoes, anything to escape that intense, green gaze. "What's there to explain? She's your fiancé, isn't she? I understand perfectly."

I'm just a fling on the side. You went slumming for a while, but when push comes to shove, you'll marry someone like you. Someone from your world.

Someone you deserve.

He tilted my chin up with a gentle hand. "Look at me."

"I don't want to," I whispered. Tears threatened to fall at any moment, and I didn't want him to see me like this. Weak. Because of him.

"Look at me, Isabeau." His voice was harsh now, brooking no further argument.

My eyes flicked upward, captured by his gaze. To my surprise, he didn't look angry at all, but instead his eyes pleaded with me.

"She's just a friend of the family. My mother has been trying to set me up with her since prep school, but I never agreed to it. I'm with *you*, Isa. Not her. Never her."

I wanted to believe him. Wanted to fall into his arms right then and there, but it all seemed too easy. *Too good to be true.*

"Then why are you going with her?"

He stared down at me, his brow furrowing. "It's a dinner party my family is throwing. I have to go, or it won't look right. Business associates will be there."

He leaned in and kissed me slowly, his lips hot on mine. My head buzzed, my thoughts a hopeless jumble. His mouth found my neck, his hand winding in my hair and pulling it tight. My breath hitched, my body responding to his touch. His tongue flicked over my collar bone, and I moaned softly.

"Come with me," he said, his breath tickling my ear. "Let me introduce you to my family, Isa."

I sighed against him, my anxiety melting as his body

pressed against mine. I squirmed against him, my needy clit finding his rock hard thigh.

"You want me to go?"

His low laugh sent shivers down my spine. His thigh rubbed against me, making me gasp.

"You're mine. I can show you off as I please, little slave."

He grabbed my ass, lifting my leg over his, grinding me harder. I was on fire for him, and still wet from our play in the office, before all of this doubt and fear. Mr. Drake nibbled at my neck as he rubbed me against him, my pussy throbbing with arousal even through the layers of clothing separating us.

"Say you'll join me. Be my date tonight."

He kissed me, and I opened beneath him, sighing as his tongue danced over mine. Jolts of pleasure raced through me as I rode him, my hips undulating as he moved against me. I gasped as he bit my lip.

"I will," I breathed.

"Good," he said, grinning. "Now cum for me, Isa."

He squeezed my ass, grinding me down harder, and I gave in, letting go right then and there, trembling in his arms as my orgasm crashed over me. I think I called out his name, my fingernails digging into his shoulders as I shuddered against him, my pussy clenching again and again.

I was grinning when I finally came back down to earth. Mr. Drake cocked an eyebrow at me.

"I think I'm going to need some fresh panties before I meet your mother."

He kissed my lips and smirked at me. "I'll have the driver stop on the way."

***

Mr. Drake and I met Lex and Veronica in the lobby. I tried not to glare at the owner of the high, breathy voice I'd heard earlier from my position under the desk. The Future

Mrs. Drake was a thin, icy blonde with a lip glossed smile glued onto her face. It faltered when she saw me step out of the elevator, but snapped back like rubber when she saw Mr. Drake. Lex was leaning against a marble column, looking positively bored. His black eyes twinkled when he saw me, his grin making me blush.

"Chasey, about time! I was starting to think you forgot about me." Veronica pouted, crossing her arms over her pink sheath dress, her diamond necklace shifting against her throat.

"Veronica, I'd like you to meet my assistant, Isabeau. Isabeau, Veronica. Our families have known each other since we were children."

I shook her hand more firmly than I should have, forcing a smile. "Pleasure to meet you."

"Yes, well," she said, looking me up and down. "When are we leaving, Chasey? Are you driving?"

"Isabeau and I will be making a quick stop before we arrive. Lex, would you please take Ms. Chambers in your car?"

"Before *we* arrive?" Veronica raised a perfectly sculpted eyebrow, her cool blue eyes narrowing.

"Yes. Isa will be escorting me this evening. I hope my mother didn't mislead you, Veronica. I said I would attend, but never made any definite arrangements."

I looked up at Mr. Drake. His face was a blank mask; his emotions unreadable. Veronica ran a hand over her coiffure, and stood a little straighter.

"Of course. No problem at all. I'll see you there."

Mr. Drake took my hand and placed it in the crook of his arm before leading me out to the parking lot. His hand closed over mine, and my skin tingled at the touch. The gesture was so gentlemanly... so *protective*. I felt my cheeks heating in the crisp night air.

"Do you think she was disappointed?"

I smiled at him as he opened the car door for me.

"I can guarantee it." His lips twitched into a half grin.

I slid into my seat and straightened my skirt against the leather, my heart fluttering at the fact that this man had just chosen me over someone like that. Maybe I had nothing to worry about. Maybe this mysterious man meant exactly what he said when he claimed I was his.

***

The Bentley's headlights shone on a large, wrought-iron gate, leading to the biggest house I'd ever seen in my life. It actually looked like Mr. Darcy's manor from the Colin Firth version of Pride and Prejudice--a sprawling construction that looked more like an ancient castle than anywhere an American family would live. We were at the top of a hill, the Drake estate tucked back away from the other wealthy residences, their window-covered walls glinting in the moonlight as we drove past.

Mr. Drake rolled down his window and pressed the intercom button. "Chase Drake."

"Nice to see you again, Sir," piped the voice through the speaker. There was a quick buzz, and then the gates rolled to the side, allowing entrance to the grounds.

I sank into my seat, the enormity of what I was about to do overwhelming me. I was about to enter a party in Mr. Drake's childhood home. I was about to meet his mother. Suddenly, it was too hot in the car, my body sweating beneath the designer clothing he'd chosen for me. Would she approve of me for her son? Or would she be able to tell with just one look that I was a nobody--just some temp he decided to sleep with this week?

The car rolled forward, and I swallowed hard.

By the time we were parked, nestled next to Mercedes, BMW's, and what looked like James Bond's Aston Martin, my mouth was bone dry. Mr. Drake's hand on my leg made me jump.

"Are you okay, Isa? You look positively shaken."

"I'm fine. Really."

How could I tell a man like this that this kind of thing terrified me? That I knew I wasn't good enough? That just the sight of a house like this made me want to curl up into a ball and disappear? He would never understand. How could he, when he grew up here?

"You're not fine, Isabeau. You're missing something." His voice was low, with a hint of humor in it.

"Missing something?"

"Of course, little slave," he said, his hand caressing my throat. "Did you think I wouldn't notice?"

I sucked in a breath, the touch of this thumb over my delicate skin making me shiver with longing.

"I gave you that collar to wear, not to leave behind when you left this morning. A beautiful woman like you should always wear beautiful things."

He reached into the glove compartment and pulled out a velvet box. When he opened it, the diamonds on the platinum choker glittered in the moonlight. I looked down at my hands, clasped in my lap.

"It feels like too much."

"Isabeau." Mr. Drake tilted my chin up, forcing me to meet his gaze. "It's not too much, and it makes me happy to give it to you. Please wear it. Let the world see that you are mine."

Hesitantly, I ran a finger over the charm in the shape of a lock, caressing its edges. "Alright. But I feel silly wearing something so extravagant."

"Trust me, Isa. No one will think twice seeing it around your neck."

He brushed my hair off my shoulders and fastened it for me. His fingers trailed from the lock down the skin exposed by my blouse, before dipping beneath the silk and tracing the top of my cleavage. My body heated in response to his touch, and suddenly, I wished we didn't have to be here. That we could go straight back to his home and he could savage me in his dungeon. I moaned at the thought. Looking up into those green eyes of his, I knew he was thinking the same thing.

He drew his hand back and sighed.

"Let's go."

***

I found myself touching the necklace for reassurance as I strolled at Mr. Drake's side through the crowd of dinner guests. As if the honest-to-God butler who showed us in wasn't enough, the house itself was covered in luxuries that made my eyes pop. A fabrige egg stood on a polished silver stand next to marble statuettes in an enormous glass case, and oil paintings of who I assumed were family members lined the walls. The place reeked of old money in a way that made the hair on my neck stand on end.

What could I possibly have to say to someone who lived in a place like this? Would his family hate me right away, or would they wait until I inevitably made a fool of myself to shun me?

I closed my eyes and balled my hands into fists. *Just breathe...*

Mr. Drake's hand on my arm brought me back. "Relax, Isa. You're doing fine."

He smiled, and my heart warmed at the way his eyes crinkled ever so slightly in the corners. I wanted to stand on my tip toes and kiss him then and there, but I settled for putting my hand in his and letting him lead me through the room.

"Chase, darling. So glad you could make it after all, although I wouldn't know it from all those calls you ignored."

"Hello, Mother. You look lovely, as always."

Mr. Drake leaned over and kissed her papery cheek. She was in her sixties with silvery blonde hair swirled into an elegant up-do. Her hard, grey eyes assessed me, roaming from the top of my wavy hair down to the points of my heels, before coming back up to rest on the choker.

"Yes, well. Some of us have to keep up appearances." She touched the strand of pearls at her throat and pursed her coral lips.

Mr. Drake's hand on the small of my back was a reassuring presence.

"Mother, let me introduce you to Isabeau Willcox. Isabeau, this is Madeline Drake."

"Another one of your colleagues, Chase? Should I even bother remembering her name?" She extended her hand, and I took it out of habit, although I felt like my jaw had hit the floor at her words. "Nice to meet you, Miss Flavor-of-the-Week. Now, if you'll excuse me?'

"Mother," he began, his voice low and dangerous, but she was already waving to a guest, smiling warmly.

"Please ignore her," he growled. "She's... not easy to please."

I swallowed hard. Even dressed like this, she saw me as a nobody. *Just another one of Mr. Drake's girls. Not worth remembering.*

"I can see that."

"Isa." He clasped my hand in his, before bringing it to his lips. "I've never brought a date to this house before."

My eyes widened as I met his gaze. "Then, what did she-?"

"I've brought a few women to fundraisers and the like when I needed someone on my arm, but never here. Never to my old home. Never to meet her."

I grinned. "I can't imagine why not."

Mr. Drake laughed, the sound making my heart beat faster. "It wasn't worth it for anyone else."

Before I could wrap my head around that sentiment, a man with a tray of wine glasses approached, and then another with h'ors d'oeuvres. I sipped the wine, letting the taste roll over my tongue. It was by far the best sauvignon blanc I'd ever tasted. How did I get here, eating and drinking in a veritable castle, with people who never would have given me the time of day if I weren't on the arm of their billionaire golden boy? It was more than overwhelming. It was surreal.

Madeline tapped on her glass with a spoon, drawing

everyone's attention.

"Dinner will now be served, if you'll please follow me to the banquet room."

Her intricately beaded dress rustled as she walked, her rings clinking together as she gestured for everyone to follow. I felt underdressed in my work clothing, despite the Gucci label caressing the base of my spine, but I placed my hand on Mr. Drake's offered arm and let him lead me through the crowd. I noticed Veronica scowling at me as we passed, and suppressed a smile.

The food was exquisite. I managed to not embarrass myself with the myriad of forks and plates by keeping a close eye on what my boss was doing next to me. When he reached for the smallest fork, I reached for mine. When he placed his plate to the side, I followed suit. I made it through seven small and equally delicious courses without so much as a raised eyebrow from anyone around us, and the thought made me relax a bit.

Maybe I was almost blending in. Maybe I could traverse this strange new world after all.

After dinner, there were drinks, and after drinks, there was dancing. I thrilled when Mr. Drake extended his hand and led me out to the floor, holding me tight when the music began. It was a waltz, and I followed his lead, smiling like a schoolgirl as he twirled me in his arms. Couples surrounded us, young and old, their cocktail dresses glittering in the low light, cufflinks gleaming.

"You dance beautifully, Isa," Mr. Drake said, drawing me closer as the music changed.

Instead of the crisp waltz, sultry piano jazz now filled the space, slowing the tempo of the dancers around us.

"It's easy when I can follow your lead," I said, meeting his eyes with a smile.

His pupils darkened as he gazed down at me, his grip tightening on my waist. "I wish I could take you away from here right now. I would lead you in so much more."

He moved closer, pressing his cheek to mine, his breath

tickling my neck.

"Would you like that, little slave?"

He kissed my ear softly, the warmth of his lips on my skin momentarily taking my breath away.

"Yes," I said, leaning into him. "Yes, Sir."

"Don't you two look cozy?"

I looked up to see Alexander Smith smirking at me, his eyes traveling over my body pressed up against Mr. Drake's.

"Your mother is asking for you, Chase. But don't worry, I'll look after Miss Willcox while you're gone." He winked at me, and I frowned back. "May I cut in?"

Mr. Drake sighed and pulled back. "Duty calls," he said, giving me an apologetic look. "I'll be back as soon as I can, and then we can get out of here."

I nodded, my body feeling cold without him holding me tight. Lex held out his hand.

"Well? How about it? I haven't gotten to dance with a single beautiful woman tonight, so it would mean a lot to me."

I placed my hand in his and let him draw me close, swaying to the music. Something about his tone of voice made me wonder if he was making a joke at my expense, but I smiled up at him, not wanting to offend Mr. Drake's partner.

"I don't know if I fit the bill, but I'm happy to let you cut in."

He laughed, his black eyes full of humor. "Very good, Miss Willcox."

I couldn't help but notice how his face changed when he smiled; how his entire demeanor lightened, his white teeth dazzling against his tan complexion.

"I hope you don't think I'm forward for asking," he said, his voice low, "but are you and Chase...? Are you seeing one another?"

I felt the necklace, cool against my throat, and swallowed hard, not sure what to say. *What were we, after all? Slave and master? Boyfriend and girlfriend? Lovers?*

This wasn't exactly the kind of relationship I was used to. "Why do you ask?"

I chewed my lips and met his gaze, not wanting to give too much away. What was Mr. Drake comfortable with me talking about? Hell, what was *I* comfortable talking about?

Lex's hand moved lower on my back, and I flinched in his arms. He stopped, his fingers dangerously close to the curve of my ass.

"You are a lovely young woman, Isabeau."

His eyes were serious now, all trace of mirth long gone. But what was reflected there shocked me. Hunger, raw and obvious shone in his eyes. He pulled me closer, almost imperceptibly, but I could feel him hardening against me through the thin fabric of my skirt. My breath hitched as I met him, stare for stare. What was going on here?

"Chase Drake is a complicated man," he said, his body moving against mine to the slow rhythm of the song. "People who get close to him often seem to get hurt... I just want you to be careful."

"What do you mean?"

My voice was higher than normal, but I couldn't help it. My whole body was tensing under that stare of his, my body reacting to his touch, even though all I wanted to do was get away. But I didn't want to create a scene in the middle of Mr. Drake's mother's party.

"Has he told you about the other women he's seen, Isabeau? About how those relationships end? How they always end?"

I looked away, searching the crowd for a sign of Mr. Drake returning.

"Chase isn't the only one out there, Isabeau," he said, drawing my eyes back to his. "He isn't the only one who sees what kind of woman you are."

He pressed against me again, and I jerked back, breaking out of his grasp.

"Excuse me, I... I need a drink."

I hurried off the dance floor, toward the far end of the

room where dessert wine was being served. When I glanced back, Lex was still on the floor, grinning with his hands on his hips as if I were a mystery that needed solving. I took a glass of wine and raised it to my lips. The sweetness pouring over my tongue made me feel ill, and I put it back down.

Out of the corner of my eye, I saw Mr. Drake enter, followed closely by Veronica. He said something to her, then broke away, moving toward me.

"I'm sorry that took so long. Are you ready to go, Isa?"

Veronica grinned at me as if she'd won some sort of victory, but the smile faded as I took Mr. Drake's outstretched hand in mine.

"Please. Let's get out of here."

***

I was quiet as we drove back to Mr. Drake's home, my thoughts going a mile a minute. *What was that on the dance floor? Was he seriously trying to seduce me, or warn me away?* The way I'd felt when he'd held me made me shiver at the memory. He was handsome and charming, but it was all superficial. Something about him made my skin crawl.

So why was I still thinking about what he'd said?

"What are you thinking about, Isa?"

Mr. Drake put his hand on my leg, stroking my knee with his thumb.

"Is it my mother? The way she treated you? Because I don't base who I see on her opinion."

I glanced over at him and saw his smile falter.

"I'm sorry that happened. That she said what she did."

I placed my hand on his, squeezing it softly. "Don't worry about it. I didn't expect her to like me."

Not when she's already chosen Veronica to be the Future Mrs. Drake, Daughter-in-law Extraordinaire.

"She's set in her ways. After my father passed, she grew less tolerant of anyone not like herself."

He brought my hand up to his lips, kissing my palm as

he drove through the night. "Besides, the only opinion I care about is yours. Will you stay with me tonight?"

My head swam, even though I hadn't had much to drink. But the thought of relinquishing myself into Mr. Drake's arms, of giving up my worries to a night of passion in his embrace, was too good to pass up. I needed a break from my own thoughts. I needed to give the reins of control over, even if it was just for one night.

"Yes, Sir."

***

His shirt hit the floor before he'd even closed the door to the dungeon. We were a tangle of bodies, me kissing every inch of him I could find as he ripped my new blouse, eager to get me naked. He finally closed the secret door, and held me at arm's length.

"You have been a very bad little girl, Isabeau. A very bad slave indeed."

I stared up at him, my eyes widening in surprise. "What? How?"

He reached around and slapped my bottom. "For one, forgetting the rules in here. Is that any way to address your master?"

I grinned, looking down at the floor. "No, Sir. I'm sorry, Sir."

He unzipped my skirt slowly, then slid it down off my body one inch at a time, making me step out of it. I was wearing nothing but my underwear set and heels now, and I clasped my hands in front of me, waiting for him to speak.

"Secondly, you didn't wear your collar today. I had to bring it to you, or you'd have forgotten it entirely. That is a grave mistake on your part."

He moved around me, trailing his fingers along my spine as he moved to one of his cabinets. The door creaked open as he removed a black box.

"For that, you must be punished."

He opened the box in front of me, and I saw the black leather collar lying inside of it.

"Take off the choker and put on your other collar."

I did as I was told. The leather was cool against my skin as I buckled it on, the feeling of it around my neck making my pussy tingle. I was *his* to do with as he pleased, completely at his beck and call. The thought made me moan out loud.

"Take off your underwear. I want you naked for this."

I unhooked my bra and slowly removed it, sighing as the cool air made my nipples pucker. Mr. Drake stood back, watching from the shadows of the doorway, his eyes roaming over my curves. I hooked my thumbs into my panties and slid them down my legs. I stumbled a little as my heel caught in the lace, and felt my face heating with embarrassment.

"God, you're beautiful," he breathed, stepping back into the light. His hand went between my legs, his fingers sliding deftly between my folds. "And already so wet. Does the thought of punishment turn you on, little slave? Are you disobeying me on purpose?"

His other hand wrapped around my throat, his thumb caressing my skin even as he dipped a finger inside of me.

"Yes, Sir. No, Sir."

"What am I to do with a slave you won't wear her collar, hmm? Don't you want to feel that you're mine? To know you're wearing my collar under everyone's noses?"

I gasped as he slid another finger into my wetness, making me squeeze around him.

"Yes, Sir. I do, Sir."

"Then, I'll have to make sure you've learned your lesson, little girl."

He removed his fingers, and I groaned as they slipped out of me. He brought his hands to his mouth, making me watch as he slowly sucked them between his lips, tasting my arousal. My body throbbed, so turned on, I could barely stand it. He licked his lips.

"I love the way you taste, but do you know what I like even better?"

I shook my head, my eyes still locked on his beautiful mouth, the corner of his lip still shining with my juices.

"No, Sir."

"Spanking that little ass of yours until it's bright red. Come with me."

He led me by the throat to a strange, angled block, almost like a bench, before bending me over it. My backside was straight up in the air, my heels touching the ground. My breasts pressed against the leather of the bench, my head pointing toward the floor. Mr. Drake knelt before me and secured each of my wrists in leather cuffs attached to the frame. He then walked around behind, and I tensed, unable to turn and follow him with my eyes.

His hands were on my ankles, and soon I felt leather tightening around each of them, too, spreading my legs and binding me to this naughty piece of furniture. I couldn't struggle, couldn't escape--my ass was in a perfect position for him to do anything he wanted, and I couldn't resist.

Not that I'd want to anyway, I thought, and grinned to myself. What was my master going to do now that he had me right where he wanted me?

"Now, I'm going to give you the spanking you deserve, and then I'm going to take this ass of yours, to drive the lesson home. Understood?"

He ran his thumb over my pucker, and I gasped, fear and arousal warring within me.

"Yes... Sir."

He toyed with me, running his hands over my ass, kneading the flesh before tracing my back entrance with curious fingers. My core was on fire, aching for him to fill me, but at the same time, I wondered what it would feel like. Would it be like his finger, or would it hurt? Would I enjoy it?

As if sensing my thoughts, Mr. Drake's hands went still.

"Has anyone taken your ass before, little slave?"

"N-no... no, Sir."

There was a sound behind me like a moan, and I wondered what he was thinking.

"Then I'll be the first."

I heard him moving, then suddenly his mouth was between my cheeks, his tongue running over my slick folds before lapping at my asshole. I yelped in surprise, then groaned, as the sensation washed over me. Shame colored my cheeks at the thought of what he was doing, but then his tongue began to probe me, making my muscles relax and heat, and I didn't care how dirty I'd once thought this was. I was a new Isabeau, after all. A wild woman who did things she'd never thought she could do.

And this new Isabeau wanted more.

Mr. Drake's hot mouth left me, the cold air making me tense again at his absence.

"You'll get 30 for your misbehavior, and then I'll take that tight, virgin ass of yours. Now, count them off."

"Yes, Sir," I said, breathless at the thought.

"If you miss a number, I'll start over."

I could practically hear the grin in his voice, knowing that he had me like this, totally in his control, my body squirming and ready beneath him. His hand came down hard, the *smack* reverberating throughout the dungeon.

"One," I gasped, the sting making my eyes water.

His hand came down again on the other cheek, the bite of pain making my arousal leak onto my thighs.

"Two!"

If I closed my eyes, I could still imagine his mouth on me, licking my most intimate places...

Another slap, then another. "Three... Four!"

He hit the same spots now, the impact of his hand driving the sharp sting deeper into me, my body coming alive beneath the onslaught.

"Five... uhhh... Six!"

He went faster, as if trying to trip me up, spanking my cheeks one after the other, harder and faster. I felt the pain melting into something intoxicating, my pussy throbbing along with each smack. I cried out the numbers again and again, feeling like I was on the edge of pleasure from just this, the simple surrender of this one act.

When I called "Thirty!" out, I was out of breath, my body glowing with delicious pain, even as I lay, bound and ready for what was to come.

I heard a bottle cap open, and jumped against my restraints when cool gel hit my pucker. Mr. Drake smoothed the lubricant around the outside of my hole before dipping a finger past the tight ring of muscle. I groaned, my ass stinging where his hand rested against it.

"I hope you've learned what it is to be mine, little slave. I hope that spanking drove it home for you, but just in case... I'm going to fuck the lesson into you as well."

I was panting now, his finger torturing me as he moved it achingly slow, in and out, in and out, pushing further into my ass each time. He added a second finger, and I felt the stretch, my body protesting at first, then squeezing around him as he readied me. I needed him. Needed to be filled, to be owned. To be satisfied.

"Now, little slave. Take me inside of you. Take it all in..."

I bit my lip as I felt the tip of his thick cock press against my opening. My arms tightened against the leather cuffs, wanting to reach back and stroke him, or at least see what was happening. But I was totally helpless. Totally his.

"Relax, baby," he whispered. "Relax, and push out."

I took a deep breath, and let it out slowly, willing myself to relax as I did so. I pushed out like he instructed, and whimpered as the head of his shaft slipped inside of me. A twinge of pain ran through me, my ass feeling like a fiery ring stretching around him.

"Shhh," he said, stroking my back. "You'll adjust."

I focused on my breathing, my breasts heaving against the leather. A tingle started then, overriding the discomfort, melting it into something new and utterly sensual. I felt my body accepting him into me, and he pushed a little, working himself in one inch, then stopping, letting me get used to the feeling. The pain was turning itself inside out, becoming pleasure, and I was singularly focused on the sensation of him filling me up in a way no one had before. I was aware of each twinge of feeling, each tiny movement of his body in mine.

He eased back, and I gasped, this time at the delicious friction. His shaft inched its way back into me, teasing me slowly as I relaxed around it. A tear rolled down my face, but not from pain. He was driving me insane, when all I wanted him to do was drive into me and make me come apart.

"That's it. Good girl. That's my good girl. *Fuck*, you are so tight..."

He gripped my ass, his touch on my tender cheeks making me moan. He pushed into me again, but this time didn't stop, burying himself balls-deep inside of my ass. He groaned loudly behind me, squeezing me tightly, and I knew he was as excited as I was.

"Please," I begged.

"What's that, slave? Please what?"

His hand came down on my ass with a *smack*, and he began pulling out inch by inch.

"Please! Please fuck me, Sir."

There was a hiss of breath, and then he thrust back into me, making my whole body burn.

"Please fuck you? You want me to fuck your little ass?"

He gripped my hips hard, his fingers biting into my skin, and began pistoning in and out, moving agonizingly slowly as he pulled back a few inches, then rammed home again.

"Yes! Oh, God, yes, Sir. Yes, please, Sir..."

I wanted to claw at the bench, to push back against him, but I was held fast. I could only wait... and feel.

"Don't say I'm not good to you," he said as he picked up the pace.

The feeling of his thick cock stretching me, rubbing me from the inside out, stuffing me fuller than I'd ever experienced was driving me to the edge, but I couldn't quite get there. I was all wanting, with no way to get what I needed. I drove my clit forward, hoping it would bump the bench, but the angle of the contraption made it impossible.

His hand came down on my ass again, making me cry

out. "I'm the one who decides when you cum, little slave. Trust your master."

I moaned as he drove into me harder, his hands spreading me open to him so he could hit me even deeper. My nipples scraped against the bench, my body a symphony of nerve endings firing all at once. Then, his hand was beneath me, lifting my hips, his rough finger finding my greedy nub.

He fucked me harder, his finger pad rubbing me with each thrust of his hips. I was gasping, my ass squeezing around him in time with the electric jolts of pleasure he was drawing out of me with each stroke of his hand.

"Cum for me now, Isa. Cum for me hard."

I screamed, giving myself over to what had been slowly building inside of me since we burst through that door. My legs stiffened, my ankles pulling at the restraints as my body convulsed, my ass milking him even as he kept thrusting, pushing himself inside of me again and again and again. I rode his hand, my back arching even as my fists balled beneath me, my fingernails cutting into my palms.

"Oh, God... Isa..." he said hoarsely above me.

He smacked my ass one last time, and then drove himself into me, tensing as he held himself still. I felt him cum inside of me, his shaft twitching as I trembled around him, still reeling from the power of my orgasm. His fingers brushed over me again and again, until finally, I went limp against the bench, spent and sweaty and unable to take any more.

His hand pulled away, and then he was gently backing out of me, the tip of his cock making me groan as it stretched me one last time before slipping past the rim. I lay there, sleepiness threatening to spirit me away while I heard the sounds of Mr. Drake washing up in a dark alcove at the side of the room.

A warm, soft washcloth ran gently over my body, cleansing me from behind. I sighed as he worked, carefully washing my folds and cheeks, before finally patting me down with a soft towel. Then, he was kneeling before me, undoing the cuffs from my wrists, and I realized I could stand.

He helped me up, and I stood, feeling limp and boneless from our lovemaking. He kissed me gently, cupping my face in his hands.

"Come to bed with me?"

I nodded, and kissed him back, losing myself in the simplicity of being with him, here, like this, away from prying eyes and disapproving mothers. Away from the too-expensive collar and the staff waiting to drive him wherever he wished. Just here. Just us.

He carried me up the stairs to his room like he hadn't just exhausted himself, then lay me in his bed before climbing in beside me. I snuggled into him as he wrapped his arms around me, noticing with a smile how I seemed to fit so perfectly into that space between his pec and his shoulder. Like it was made just for me.

But when the lights went out, I stayed awake, staring out at the city lights, far below the bedroom windows. Did I fit into any other aspect of Chase Drake's life, or was it just my own foolish hopes that kept me coming here? Did I fit into that party tonight, or, worse, into that long line of brokenhearted women Lex warned me about?

Did I fit that spot, or was I just as out of place as I felt when I stood next to him in those borrowed clothes?

And if I didn't, what did that mean for Chase Drake and I?

7 AT HIS DESIRE

I awoke from dreams of rough lovemaking in Mr. Drake's dungeon and stretched my arms over my head, yawning peacefully. I could still feel where his hands had gripped my hips the night before, and traced the skin he'd touched with relish. The sun was just coming up over the hill, the floor-to-ceiling windows tinting themselves to keep out the unwelcome light.

I sat up, realizing the other side of the bed was empty, the red sheets crumpled and cold. Where was Mr. Drake? I'd hoped to catch him sleeping just this once... to get a glimpse of him beside me, vulnerable and completely mine. To see him, just once, when he wasn't in total control.

No such luck.

I should have known that a man like him always rises early.

I slipped a silk robe over my shoulders and padded down the hall to the stairway, hoping to find him at breakfast, but as I neared the second floor landing, raised voices met my ears. I stopped just shy of Mr. Drake's study, hesitating in the shadows. The door was open just a crack, but the male voice floating through the doorway was all too familiar. Lex Smith was here, his sharp voice echoing through the hallway.

"We've got no other choice, Chase! Honestly, what else

do you think we should do? We've got to make an impression on these people, or we'll lose them."

"I thought you said it wasn't anything to worry about? That the losses were minimal?"

"So, I understated the issue a bit. That's not the point. We've got to build investor confidence."

"We can't afford-"

"We can't afford *not* to!"

I heard Mr. Drake sigh, and imagined him running a hand through his hair. I felt like I was intruding on a private moment, an eavesdropper who had no business listening in. I debated with myself for a moment, then turned and snuck downstairs toward the kitchen. If Mr. Drake wanted me to know what was going on, he'd tell me himself. I wasn't about to break his trust.

After a hot cup of coffee and one of the chef's delicious omelets, Mr. Drake appeared around the corner. For the briefest of moments, he looked exhausted, his green eyes dulled with worry. Then he saw me, and smiled.

"So, you're up after all. Excellent. I need you to go back to your apartment and pack your things."

I lowered my fork. "Good morning to you, too."

He leaned over and kissed my hair, his expression softening. "Good morning, Isa. I wish I weren't in such a hurry, but I have work to do. Quickly. We need to put together a weekend getaway for the investors and members of the board, and we need to do it now."

He grabbed a fresh baked croissant from a basket on the counter and toyed with it absentmindedly. "Hopefully they haven't already gotten wind..."

I put my hand on his arm, and he looked at me, as if startled that I was still there.

"What can I do to help?"

He frowned, his eyes appraising me. "I need to call everyone on the investor list, and set up three days and two nights of entertainment to occupy them all. Mr. Smith offered his parents' hotel and casino as a possible location."

I took a deep swig of coffee, and stood up. "No problem. Give me the names, and I'll take care of the rest."

His lips twisted into a half smile, his eyes twinkling incredulously. "Isa, are you sure--"

"I used to put together events for my grandmother's charity all the time. I've got this."

He raised an eyebrow, obviously needing more.

"She built a halfway house for problem teens, but could no longer handle running it when she fell ill. I was the only one who could help out, so I guess you could say I learned on the job. I know a thing or two about organizing events for wealthy benefactors." I smiled up at him. "Trust me. I can help you, if you let me."

He ran a hand over his chin, as if absorbing my words. "Well, aren't you just full of surprises?"

I put a hand on my hip. "Are you going to let me take care of this, or are we going to stand here all day?"

He laughed then, the sound making my heart do a back flip.

"Get ready, and I'll drive you." He pulled me close, kissing me hard. "And if we finish early, maybe you can get tied up at the office..."

I laughed with him, and he smacked me playfully on the rear. I'd definitely have to work quickly.

***

I sat on the floor of Mr. Drake's office, surrounded by a fan of index cards, his laptop, and a fistful of hotel brochures. My ear was aching around my blue tooth headset from the day's worth of phone calls, but I grinned as I surveyed all that I'd accomplished.

I looked up as Mr. Drake entered, closing the door behind him.

"Is there anything you need? How's it going?"

There was a wrinkle above the bridge of his nose that

only showed when he was anxious. I wanted to jump up and kiss it away, but instead, I pulled up the page of notes I had on the computer.

"Everything's booked, and 20 out of 22 guests have RSVP'd in the positive, along with their spouses. This weekend is going to be a huge success. No one can pass up an all-expenses paid corporate bash thrown by **The** Chase Drake." I grinned up at him, and blew a piece of hair out of my face where it had fallen out of my bun.

He shook his head, a smile replacing the pinched look of almost-panic he had been wearing. "I don't know what I'd do without you. How did you manage to pull all this off?"

He gave me a hand, pulling me to my feet.

"Didn't you know I'm a genius?"

"I always suspected as much."

We stared at one another, the laughter fading, replaced by something else entirely. He grabbed my hair, tilting my head back, and I let my breath out slowly, my whole body suddenly very aware that we were alone. His mouth met mine, hot and urgent. I moaned softly as he deepened the kiss, teasing my tongue with his.

"I'm going to need you, Isabeau. With me. This weekend."

He kissed me again, slowly, his lips on mine making me quake with longing. He pulled away and looked into my eyes.

"Please say you'll come?"

I smiled up at him. "I'd love to. As long as you promise not to work me too hard."

His hand slipped up under my skirt. He ran a finger over the crotch of my panties, tracing my lips through the lace. "I will promise no such thing."

I shivered beneath his touch. "I'm all yours, Sir."

***

The next couple of days passed in a whirlwind of activity. I finally went home to my lonely little apartment to see that my mail was piling up and my one houseplant was getting crispy around the edges. I watered it, marveling at how quickly my life had changed in such a short period of time.

I changed out of my new clothes and stepped into the bathroom for a shower. The diamonds on my choker winked at me in the mirror. I'd become so used to wearing Mr. Drake's collar, I'd almost forgotten to take it off. I ran my fingertip over the tiny lock charm nestled in the hollow of my throat. I could practically feel his hands in my hair as he fastened it on...

I stepped into the shower with the choker still in place and sighed as the water poured over me.

***

Later, Mr. Drake sent a car and a note insisting I go shopping for the weekend ahead, and although I grumbled at the expense, I had to admit, I had nothing to wear. The clothing in my closet wouldn't impress a J.C. Penney executive, much less the investors of Drake & Smith. I let myself be driven about, packages piling up in the trunk of the Rolls Royce and tried to tamp down the feeling of unease rising inside of me with each stop.

Was I ever going to get used to this? I imagined guilt bubbling up inside of me like hot lava.

Just breathe, Isabeau. So what if that dress is worth more than all the furniture in your apartment? I giggled nervously in the back of the car, and put a hand over my mouth when the driver cocked an eyebrow at me in the rearview mirror.

I'd been in the office several times arranging last minute details, but hadn't seen Mr. Drake for more than a moment or two. He'd been locked away pouring over the books with the accounting staff behind the CFO's back, hoping to find God-knows-what before the big event.

He entered his office just long enough to change his shirt and steal a kiss from me before heading back downstairs, but I felt the stress pouring off him like steam from a radiator.

I recalled the words I'd overheard between him and Lex days before, and wondered... What exactly was going on?

How bad were these losses he'd mentioned? Was Mr. Drake in serious trouble?

I chewed the cap of my pen. If I could make his problems disappear, I would in a minute. But for now, I was glad I could at least take the detail work of this weekend off his plate. I had to admit, it felt good to be needed. To be trusted with something so important.

I closed the lap top and stood up. I'd done all I could for now. The rest was up to him.

***

The driver held the car door open, and I stepped out, fidgeting in my red satin dress. I thanked the man, and walked to the gilded double-doors of the Titan Hotel, feeling naked in my sleeveless little number. Two men in full livery swept the doors open for me with a bow, and I nodded to them nervously as I walked through.

I'd heard of this hotel before, but had never even been to this part of the city, much less set foot inside the gleaming, modern structure. The Smith family had built this hotel and casino to cater to the super rich, a place where luxury and exclusivity were guaranteed. I blew out a shaky breath, and stood up a little straighter. Just because I couldn't afford a snow globe in the gift shop didn't mean I didn't belong.

Sure, Isabeau. Just keep telling yourself that. Maybe one day, you'll even believe it.

The choker shifted around my neck, and I sighed. I wasn't in this alone.

I moved through the lobby, my heels click-clacking on the veined marble. Water sculptures framed the check in and concierge desks, while the entire back wall housed an enormous aquarium. I moved toward it, marveling at the way the light from the water danced across the floor, mirroring the movement of the colorful fish housed within. The light dimmed for a moment as a shark swam by. I jumped and backed away. My back collided with something hard, but before I could turn around, strong hands clamped down on my arms.

"You look breathtaking this evening, Miss Willcox."

The sound of Lex Smith's oily voice made goose bumps rise on my flesh. I pulled out of his grasp, and heard him chuckle.

"Thank you."

He grinned at me like a wolf, his eyes wandering over the drape of my satin dress all the way down to my exposed legs. I wanted to cover up under that stare, but wouldn't give him the satisfaction.

"I'm glad you came to this little get together. I've been thinking about you." He brushed back his dark hair, his silver cufflink gleaming in the light from the aquarium.

"Oh?" I didn't like where this was going, but I didn't want to be rude.

"Absolutely," he said, his voice lowering to a purr. "I hope we'll get another chance to dance, you and I."

I didn't know what to say. The last thing I wanted were his hands on me, but I didn't want to cause a scene by telling him what I really thought about him. Not when this weekend was so important to the company. I backed away just as the elevator doors slid open on the other side of the lobby.

"Lex," Mr. Drake said. "I hope I'm not interrupting. Mind if I steal Isabeau away?"

If I could have leapt into his arms at that moment, I would, but instead settled for beaming at him.

Lex shot me another look, dark and full of promises. His lips twitching into a lopsided grin. "See you later, then."

I repressed a shudder. What did he want from me, anyway?

Mr. Drake's hand clasped mine, and I tore my eyes away. He led me into the elevator, his thumb caressing me. When the doors closed, he turned to me, looking me over with appreciation.

"You're so beautiful, Isa... That dress is simply stunning

on you."

He held my hand to his lips and kissed my palm, his green eyes capturing me. I licked my lips, my body heating at his touch. I wished we could be alone now, instead of going to this party. I wanted the magnetic Mr. Drake all to myself.

"You're not so bad yourself. Sir."

His sharp intake of breath told me the word had its desired effect. His eyes burned with hunger, and, standing there in a James Bond tuxedo, his wavy hair falling perfectly around his face, I wanted nothing more than to rip off those clothes and make love to him here and now.

"Watch out, Isa. I may just take you over my knee in front of all the investors and give you the spanking you deserve."

I laughed, but his look told me he might not be joking. The doors slid open.

"Come."

He slipped my arm through his and led me out into the hotel's opulent banquet room. My eyes widened as I took in the scene before me. Men and women draped in finery mingled among trays of delicacies and champagne, diamonds and pearls shining in the firelight from a wall-to-wall fireplace on the far side of the room. The walls were covered in sprawling murals depicting the Greek gods, and I stifled a grin. *How appropriate to place the richest of the rich among the gods.*

I'm sure the guests loved this place the Smith family built just for them.

I snagged a glass of champagne and took a sip.

Mr. Drake squeezed my hand. "I have to make the rounds before dinner. Thank God I have you here, or I don't think I could make it. Smiling at these people for three hours straight when all I want is to take you back to the room and do unspeakable things..."

I choked, trying not to spit my drink.

"Look alive, Miss Willcox," Mr. Drake said, chuckling softly.

He steered me over to a balding man and his plump wife

and smoothly made his introductions. I took another swig and smiled politely.

It was going to be a long night.

***

"I have a surprise for you," he whispered to me, nuzzling my neck as we rode the elevator to the penthouse suite.

"Mmm?" I wrapped my hands in his hair as he nibbled my ear, my heartbeat pounding with each touch of his lips.

We'd wined and dined the night away, and now relief flooded through me knowing that at least this night had gone as planned. Everything had been organized to perfection, and the board members and investors seemed to be enjoying themselves.

The elevator shuddered to a halt, and I squealed as Mr. Drake scooped me up into his arms.

"I think you're going to enjoy it, little slave," he said. "Do you trust me?"

He set me down just long enough to unlock the door at the end of the hall, then threw me over his shoulder again. I giggled against his tuxedo jacket, the wine and the intoxicating smell of his cologne making me feel giddy.

He kicked the door shut and tossed me onto the bed so hard that I bounced. I glanced around, my breath catching at the view, visible from the huge marble balcony attached to the suite. Stars winked at me from the clear night sky, and I grinned. Even when he traveled, Mr. Drake had to be on top of the world.

"You didn't answer me. Do you trust me, Isa?"

He towered over me at the foot of the bed, looking sexy as hell with his tuxedo shirt half unbuttoned, bow tie hanging askew where I'd tugged it open.

"Of course I do."

He leaned down under the bed and reemerged holding a small travel bag. "Then put this on."

I took it from him, and opened it, not sure what to expect. Part of me feared it would be another expensive dress, but I smiled at what I saw. A black, padded blindfold. It was perfect.

My body tingled all over as I slid it down over my eyes, securing it around the back of my head.

"Can you see anything?"

"No, Sir."

I felt him near me, but my world was now as black as pitch. The blindfold molded itself to the contours of my face, sealing out all light. He snapped his fingers an inch away from my ear, and I jumped with a little shriek.

"Good girl. I think you'll agree, it's more fun if you're honest with me..."

Hands caressed me through my dress, teasing as they ran down my ribcage, stopping just before squeezing my breasts.

"Hold your arms out at your sides and lie back, little slave."

I let him gently push me down until my head hit the pillow and both arms were stretched out like a cross. I heard a rustling near my head, but held still, waiting with bated breath to discover what my master had planned for me. Something silky wrapped around my wrist, then tightened, stretching my arm out. I heard soft footfalls on the carpet, and then my other wrist was being bound, tied in place with something strong but soft. One of his neckties, maybe? I gave an inquisitive yank, but I was held firm to the bedposts, helpless to escape.

"Now, you're mine to do with as I please. The question is... what am I going to do first?"

His low chuckle sent shivers down my spine.

There was silence for a few endless moments, stretching out until I couldn't stand it. I strained to hear him, to figure out where he was. I pictured him staring at me, bound beneath him, plotting how he could drive me crazy.

I heard a rasping noise from the edge of the bed, like metal sliding over metal, and my body tensed.

"Let's get these clothes off you. I want to see that beautiful body of yours."

Something cool and hard grazed the inside of my thigh, and I sucked in a breath, pulling at my bonds. Fear sliced through me, irrational but so real it was palpable. What was he doing?

"Shhh, little slave. Hold still."

There was a sharp, metallic *snip*, and I felt the material of my dress give way, the satin sliding down my leg.

Oh, God. He's going to cut my clothes off. Picturing large metal shears anywhere near my naked body sent pins and needles running through me. But if I trusted anyone with my safety, it was my Mr. Drake. I held as still as I could, trying not to freak out.

I whimpered as he dragged the blade of the scissors upward, teasing me, before slicing through more of my dress. My nerves felt like they were on fire as the metal moved upward, the cold steel tickling as it moved toward my panties. Arousal warred with anxiety as the *snip, snip, snip* moved closer.

My breathing was ragged by the time I felt the scissors' edge work beneath the thin lace. The metal moved slowly, oh-so-carefully, working its way beneath the crotch until I felt the dull edge caress my lower lips.

"Oh, God..." I said, my voice high and strained.

One slice, and the fabric fell away. I realized then I'd been holding my breath, and let it out slowly.

"You naughty thing," Mr. Drake said, his voice a low rumble. "You're soaking wet already."

The scissors snapped down, and one side of my panties ripped apart beneath the blades, then the other. The top half fell away, and the scissors moved upward, caressing my stomach and making me gasp.

I felt my dress shredding open, the sound of the satin parting whispering in the darkness. I tried not to move, but my chest heaved with each breath. When the scissors reached the place between my breasts, they stopped. I knew Mr.

Drake must be enjoying this, watching me tremble beneath him. The thought made me wish I could take off the blindfold and end this game, but another enjoyed the sweet torture far too much to stop.

The scissor blades snapped together, and the rest of the dress fell apart, exposing my bare breasts, for I hadn't worn a bra tonight. I felt my nipples draw tight under the stare I couldn't see, but could feel with every piece of my being.

I was his.

There was another sound of movement, and I felt him draw back. The carpet rustled, and there was a tinkling noise, a clinking of something against glass. Then, I smelled his cologne, felt his heat, and knew he stood over me, even though he didn't say a word.

I cried out when the ice cube touched my nipple.

Mr. Drake circled it gently as I mewled beneath him, and I could practically hear him smiling. He lifted it away, and I felt his cool breath blowing on my bud, making it tighten, and my pussy tingle in response. He trailed the ice across the other, then brought it up to run across my lips. I opened my mouth, and he teased me with it, letting me suck it a little before taking it away and running it down the curve of my throat. I shivered.

When he traced the line of my belly, I was squirming beneath him, the cold stinging me, but the anticipation, the wanting, the cruelest thing of all. I bit my lip when the ice touched the sensitive bud between my legs, and tried not to scream as he began moving it in small, deliberate circles.

"Please..." I whimpered.

He held the ice still, making me burn beneath him. "Please, what?"

"Please, Sir," I breathed. "Please, *Sir!*"

He laughed, the sound making me arch into his touch. The ice moved lower, tracing my folds, making me writhe on the bed sheets.

"Do you want my cock now, little slave?"

"Yes! Oh, God, please... Yes, Sir..."

The ice lifted off my aching sex. I heard the sound of a buckle and lifted my hips, searching for him with my body. A hand on my stomach pressed me back down, pinning me onto the bed. Then, he was pushing my legs apart, spreading me open, and I felt the weight of him lower onto me. I cried out wordlessly, wanting him inside of me, wanting him to fuck me already, instead of leaving me needy and burning beneath him. I yanked on my restraints, straining toward him, but couldn't budge, the silk tightening against my wrists.

He pressed into me, aligning himself carefully. Then, his cock rammed into me in one sure stroke, and I screamed, my head slapping back against the pillow. I squeezed his hips with my thighs, wanting to be closer to him, to hold him, even as he ground into me, his pubic hair tickling my clit.

"I love how much you want me," he said, pulling out slowly, before thrusting home once again.

I bucked up to meet him, my body humming, every cell was alive, every nerve firing. His lips captured mine, his kiss taking my breathe away. He stroked into me, and I moaned into him, his tongue matching the rhythm of our lovemaking.

He gripped my ass, lifting my hips off the bed so he could hit me even deeper, pulling me to him with each thrust. My toes curled, gripping at the sheets as my wrists strained above me. I suckled on his tongue, wanting all of him, wanting as much as he would give me, my lower lips squeezing him as we collided together again and again.

"Cum for me, Isabeau..."

He gathered me in his arms, my back lifting off the bed as he supported me. I gasped against his lips, feeling him in every part of me as my pleasure crested. I came as he commanded, convulsing around him as he held me close. He groaned, too, and I felt him inside of me, filling me up, sharing my joy as we both found completion.

We lay there a long while, him holding me, bodies still joined, our sweat mingling between us. When he finally pulled away and untied me, he left the blindfold on. He lay beside me, and I curled onto his chest, the darkness making me feel safe and warm. Maybe that was why I had the courage to ask what I did.

"Why me?"

It was the question that had nagged me from the start.

"Why am I so different?"

Silence fell, except for the sound of our breathing and the beating of my own heart, loud in my ears. Then, he spoke.

"Because you see me as a man."

I wrinkled my forehead, his meaning escaping me.

"Not as a CEO or a boss or a wallet full of money... You see me for what I am, Isa. Just a man. Just Chase Drake... And I love you for that."

I pulled the blindfold off, letting it tangle in my hair. He was staring at the ceiling, his jaw set. I touched his face, turning his gaze to mine. I leaned up and kissed him softly, my lips brushing over his.

"I love you, too."

We didn't say another word that night, lying in one another's arms until sleep finally claimed us both. We didn't have to.

***

The next day moved at a break-neck pace.

Mimosas and morning golf soon segued into horseback riding for the ladies and Scotch and cigars for the men. Presentations to the well-lubricated and entertained board members went off without a hitch. Meetings transitioned into massages at the hotel spa, then h'ors d'oeuvres and cocktails by the pool.

By the time evening came, I was exhausted, tipsy, and aching for the weekend to be over and life to get back to normal, but there was still one more event before I could crash onto Mr. Drake's bed and let my exhaustion take over. There was a high stakes poker game tonight that Mr. Drake said would seal the deal with the investors.

Apparently if there's one thing rich men love more than drinking, it's gambling grotesque amounts of money. All of the most important people would be there, and I was to be on the boss' arm, at least for a hand or two. Then, I could make my escape, and wait for him under the covers.

Mr. Drake was already in his tux when I emerged from the bathroom in my short, black cocktail dress. He gave the lock charm on my choker a gentle tug, and kissed me.

"Aren't you going to wish me luck?"

"Do you need it?" I raised an eyebrow at him, and grinned.

We walked arm in arm to a private room in the back of the casino that looked like something out of a spy movie. Lex Smith sat at the table sharing a laugh with a pasty older man over some off-color joke. I hesitated, but Mr. Drake urged me toward the table. I took my seat next to him, but kept my eyes averted. The last thing I wanted was to do was gain Lex's attention again.

Wives and girlfriends came in, chatting together as the cards were dealt, some hanging back at the bar, and a couple joining in on the wagering.

I was only half paying attention when Mr. Drake slid a small pile of chips forward.

"I'll raise you to twenty five."

Lex was one of the two who hadn't folded yet. His eyes bored into Mr. Drake's as they stared one another down. Mr. Drake leaned back, and traced his bottom lip casually with one finger, looking as cool as ice.

"Do you call?"

"Come on, Lex. You can't let him beat you in the first hand," the fat man next to him said. He laughed, the sound ending with a guttural hack.

Lex shot him a dark look before pushing his own chips forward. "Fine. I'll call."

The other man folded, shaking his head.

"Show them," Lex said, leaning in.

Mr. Drake laid down his hand. Three of a kind. Kings.

Lex swore under his breath. He only had a pair of nines.

While the dealer shuffled, I leaned over and whispered in Mr. Drake's ear. "Why was he so mad about losing twenty five dollars?"

"Twenty five thousand, Isa. The ante's ten thousand per hand."

He grinned wickedly at me as the blood drained out of my face.

"Oh," I said, my voice no more than a squeak.

Everyone ante'd up again, and all of a sudden, I felt rather faint. I squeezed Mr. Drake's arm and left his side, moving toward the bar with the other women. After a stiff shot of whiskey, one of the wives put her hand on mine.

"First time?"

I nodded, giving her a shaky smile.

"You'll get used to it. Henry usually loses, but it's never too bad. Usually no more than two hundred thousand. Try not to worry."

I nodded again, lips shut tight, trying not to let my jaw drop to the floor.

"Besides, honey," she said. "Chase usually cleans everyone out, anyway."

***

After a few more hands, I felt like I'd stayed long enough, and worked my way back around to Mr. Drake's side. I whispered to him that I was heading upstairs and he smiled and nodded.

"I'm going to take this last hand from Lex, and I'll be up soon," he said.

"Sounds good."

I looked up and saw Lex watching us, an inscrutable look in his eyes that made me nervous. I excused myself, and worked my way toward the elevator bank. All of the day's drinking was catching up with me, and I concentrated hard on not falling off my high heels as I walked. When I reached the elevators, I rested my head against the cool marble above the buttons as I waited.

It seemed to take forever, but then I realized I hadn't pressed the button after all. Maybe I'm more tipsy than I thought. Truthfully, my head was starting to spin. That last shot definitely wasn't my best decision.

"Are you okay, Isabeau?"

I turned around just as the elevator chimed, the doors rolling open. Lex stood behind me, his brow furrowed.

"M' good," I said. "Going to bed."

I stumbled over the threshold of the elevator, catching myself against the back wall. I could feel the blush creeping up my neck as Lex followed me in.

"Let me make sure you get to your room in one piece. You look a little worse for wear."

I tried to protest, but he put his arm around me to steady me and hit the button for the top floor.

"No arguments. How much have you had to drink anyway?"

I noticed he seemed rock solid for someone who'd been keeping up with the investors all day, cocktail for cocktail. Then again, he probably did this a lot.

"Too much," I said, putting my hand to my forehead. The world was starting to move around me in a very unpleasant fashion. I was definitely going to pay for this in the morning.

"You should be more careful," he said.

I stared up at him, wondering exactly why he still had his arm around me, and tried to shy away.

"Don't worry, Isabeau. I'll take good care of you."

We made it to the top floor, and he helped me out, then walked me in silence to the door of the penthouse at the end of the hall, watching with mocking eyes as I fumbled in my clutch for the key card.

When I finally had it, he snatched it out of my hand.

"Let me help you get into bed," he said, his black eyes

flashing. "You're in no condition to take care of yourself."

Something about the way he was eyeing me reminded me of a fox hunting a rabbit, but he swam in my vision, and I looked away.

"I don't think so, Mr. Smith. I'll take it from here."

I tried to pry my card out of his hand, but he held it out of reach, making me move closer.

"Is that any way to thank me for helping you?" He made a tsking sound. "That's not very polite."

"C'mon, Lex. Don't mess with me," I said. My head was pounding, and I just wanted to lie down more than anything. "Thank you, okay?"

He put his finger to his chin, feigning deep thought. "I'm not sure if that's good enough. How about a goodnight kiss for your hero?"

Somewhere down the hall, I heard the elevator ping. "What? No!"

I reached for the key, but he caught my wrist, pulling me close. Panic welled up inside of me as I struggled to free myself. I didn't want to hurt one of Mr. Drake's business associates, but so help me, I would knee him in the balls if I had to. He leaned down, and I cocked my knee back to take aim. I wobbled on my one leg, and that's when Lex grabbed me. He pulled me to him and kissed me hard on the mouth, forcing his tongue past my lips.

For a moment, I was in total shock, but then my knee began it's upward journey. I missed, my knee hitting nothing but tuxedo jacket. *Fuck!*

"Lex."

The sound of Mr. Drake's voice sent a jolt of relief through me as Lex finally removed his lips from mine.

"Just what the hell do you think you're doing?" Mr. Drake stood a couple of feet away, staring at us in a way that made the relief fade as quickly as it had come. His mouth was open in a snarl, his eyes full of rage.

"Sorry you had to see that, Chase," Lex said, still holding me tight. "We thought you'd be longer."

I looked from Mr. Drake's eyes to Lex's and my heart sank. Just when I'd discovered why I was so special to him, why he was able to trust me, Lex Smith was trying to snatch it all away.

Chase Drake took a step forward and pointed at his partner, his finger stabbing the air.

"Let. Her. *Go.*"

"Please, Mr. Drake. It's not what it looks like!"

My eyes begged him to understand, to hear me out, as Lex finally let me free from his grasp. But the look he returned told me everything I needed to know.

I'd blown it with the only man I'd ever loved.

8 AT HIS WARNING

"Maybe you didn't hear me, Lex? I said, let her go."
Chase Drake stood still as a statue, his eyes blazing with
dangerous intent as he surveyed the scene before him.

Lex held me tight for a moment longer, then let out a
nervous chuckle and eased his grip.

"What's the matter, Chase? Can't keep track of your
girl?"

I jerked my arm away and stumbled away from him,
staring daggers at the man who may just have ruined one of
the best things to ever happen to me when he grabbed me
and kissed me. What was his game? Why would he do this to
his partner? Hell, why would he do this to *me?* I'd barely met
the man, but here he was trying to destroy one of the best
things to ever happen to me.

My head still swam from that last shot of whiskey, but I
braced myself against the wall of the hallway. The shock of
the past few minutes had helped clear away some of the
spinning queasiness, but I didn't trust myself not to swerve
on my heels just yet.

"It seems it's you I can't keep track of," Mr. Drake spat.
"Why, Lex? Why must you always try to ruin me? All the
women I've dated, you've tried to steal away. Didn't you

realize it just showed me how fickle they all were instead of breaking me? How they were only interested in my wealth if you could tempt them away so easily?"

Lex's eyes narrowed, the muscles in his jaw tightening. "Is it so hard to believe that someone would choose me over Chase Drake, *golden boy?*" He spat the last words, his lips pulled back in a snarl.

"I was never the golden boy, Lex. I just wasn't an asshole like you."

Lex made a noise like a growl deep in his throat. Things were definitely getting out of hand. I edged slowly away from him, hoping to escape his notice.

"What makes you think she's any different? Maybe she likes a man who takes what he wants, huh? Not some fucking boy scout..."

"Keep your hands off her," Mr. Drake said, his voice calm despite the fire in his eyes. "I won't ask you again."

"Or what? What are you gonna do? What's Chasey gonna do about it?"

Lex lurched toward me, trying to grab my wrist again, but I shrunk away. What the hell was going on between these two?

I screamed as Mr. Drake's fist connected with Lex's face.

For a moment, time seemed to slow down. I saw Lex's eyes go wide, his arms shoot up too late, just before his head snapped back with the impact. I backed up fast, giving the two men space just as Lex lashed out, his fist swinging toward Mr. Drake's stomach. Chase batted his hand aside and connected again with a vicious uppercut.

"Stop it!"

I covered my mouth with my hands, unable to look away, worried that this would get out of control, and maybe already had. Should I call for help? Or should I move in and get a couple of kicks in before the fight was over?

My head throbbed. Everything was happening so fast.

Lex landed a glancing blow on Mr. Drake's face before he was tackled into the wall. The men were grappling now, grunting and straining as each tried to gain the upper hand. Mr. Drake pushed away and squared his shoulders, ready for the attack. Lex's fist jabbed forward, but Chase was too quick for him, stepping aside, then following up with a blow to the face. Lex cried out and held a hand up, his fingers shaking. Blood poured down his chin.

"You broke my fucking nose!"

Mr. Drake bent down and ripped Lex's pocket square out of his jacket pocket. "Go clean yourself up, Lex." He tossed the handkerchief in his face. "It's over."

Lex Smith straightened up, holding the cloth to his face. Red blossomed onto the fabric as he stared at us both in a way that made my skin crawl. Then, he made a lewd gesture and slunk down the corridor, disappearing from view around the elevator banks.

I stared at Mr. Drake, not quite believing the scuffle that had just occurred between two grown men. I was torn between being appalled and impressed, especially since Lex had gotten a well-deserved beat down.

"Come, Isa. You've had a long night."

He opened the door of the penthouse suite and gestured for me to enter. I shook myself out of my state of shock and made myself move, planting one foot in front of the other until I was safely in the room and deposited on the edge of the bed.

Mr. Drake sat beside me, breathing heavily. A cut above his eye was starting to trickle red.

"You're bleeding." I grabbed a tissue from the bedside table and dabbed gently at it, stopping when he winced.

"I'll be fine."

I lowered my hand, crumpling the blood-stained Kleenex. "I'm so sorry."

I looked down at his blood, staining my fingers, and noticed my vision beginning to blur as the tears welled up.

"You didn't do anything wrong."

Mr. Drake's hand cupped my chin, bringing my eyes up to his. A hot tear rolled down my cheek, and he brushed it away, the rough pad of his thumb more tender than a kiss.

"He... He just grabbed me. I tried... I tried to knee him, but..."

"Shh, Isa. I know. I believe you."

His hand found its way into my hair, wrapping a loose curl around his fingers, caressing my neck. His gaze softened as he touched me, each stroke of his fingers through my hair releasing my tension until I felt like putty in his hands.

"Why does he hate you so much?"

The question was out before I realized it, my thoughts spoken aloud when I'd meant to keep them private.

Mr. Drake's eyes narrowed, then focused out the window, over the twinkling lights of the city.

"He and I have known each other since prep school. Did you know that? As boys we were always together, our families close from summering in neighboring cabins by the lake."

He ran his hand absently over my shoulder and down my arm as he spoke, making me shiver.

"Lex and I had so much in common, even though our personalities were so vastly different. We were both ambitious and bright, but Lex had a knack for getting into trouble. He loved pulling pranks and seeing how far he could push people before they reached their limits. His father was a hard man. An authoritarian with a penchant for drink." He looked at me and cocked an eyebrow. "Let's just say, they didn't get along."

His hands covered mine, his warmth calming me like a soothing balm.

"I was the opposite, focusing on working hard and lending a helping hand to my classmates. My mother used to say I saw the best in people... and that was the only reason Lex and I were close, but I don't know. I just thought he went too far at times. His father used to praise me in front of him, talking about the two of us to my parents like we weren't standing right there with them... Saying he wished Lex had my grades or my discipline."

He paused, sighing, and I could see how the memory still

pained him.

"It got to him. How could it not?"

"That would be terrible for any child. Being compared like that."

Mr. Drake slipped his fingers through mine and squeezed them. "He pretended that he didn't care, and for a while, I believed him. I was young and foolish. I thought we were as close as brothers when we founded this business together."

He brought my hand up to his lips and kissed it softly. "But, as you know, things change. These problems always have a way of coming to the surface."

I looked up and brushed my fingers over his jaw line, tracing the lines that gave him such masculine beauty.

"Thank you," I said.

"For what?"

"For believing in me. For believing I wouldn't betray you."

He leaned in, kissing me in a way that stole my breath away.

"Isabeau, you don't have a cruel bone in your body."

"And how would you know that?"

"Just the way you are. How you took care of your family. How you take care of me," he said. "I'll always believe in you. You make it easy."

I kissed him back, releasing my fear and doubt in that moment, letting the feel of his lips on mine wash away my worries. *He believes in me...*

I moaned, opening my mouth to him, my tongue exploring his languidly as the kiss deepened. I was lost in a haze of sensuality when he pulled away.

"Not tonight."

I leaned in, trying to capture his lips again, but he held me by my shoulders.

"Why not?"

He chuckled low in his throat. "You're drunk."

"I don't care."

His eyes flashed in warning. "I'm going to bring you some aspirin and a glass of water. Take them and hydrate, then get some sleep. That's not a request."

"But, I-"

I closed my mouth at the look on his face. He would not be disobeyed, even though I could tell by the tenting in his pants he wanted me as much as I wanted him. I wanted nothing more than to reach over and stroke him through the fabric, to unzip him slowly and reach in, wrapping my hand around his hard length. Instead, I nodded, sighing. It would do no good. Chase Drake had made up his mind.

After the water and the pills, he undressed me and lay down behind me, spooning me to him.

"You know I want you, too, Isa," he whispered, his breath tickling my ear. "But I won't make love to you when you can't properly consent."

I snuggled back against him, his words making me feel desired. Protected.

He believed me. He took care of me. He held me close to him when I needed him by my side.

I was safe in the arms of Mr. Drake.

And I knew I always would be.

***

Morning arrived, bringing with it a dull, thumping headache and a whole new batch of problems.

I rolled over and rested my head on Mr. Drake's chest, breathing in the delicious mixture of his spiced cologne and the musky smell that was all him. I ran my hand lightly through the sprinkling of hair over his pecs, listening to the steady sound of his breathing. If I could have stayed in bed with him all day, I would have, maybe watching old movies and ordering room service to ease my hangover. But I knew we still had investors to please and tasks to accomplish. I sighed with longing and pressed a kiss to his skin.

Despite the throbbing in my skull, I still wanted him,

wanted to tease him and stroke him before feeling him inside of me. I ran my hand lower, skimming over the hard planes of his abdomen before sliding below the sheets.

A rough hand grabbed my wrist, Mr. Drake's low laugh rumbling through his chest.

"And just what do you think *you're* doing?"

I laughed, too, then touched my head and winced. Too loud. Mr. Drake pulled back and smoothed my hair away from my face.

"Headache?"

I nodded. "Mmm hmm."

"Aren't you supposed to use that as an excuse *not* to make love, Isa? You seem to be doing this all wrong."

I stretched back on my pillow, letting the sheets fall off my full breasts. I smiled as his eyes traveled downward, his pupils darkening.

"But what if making love will cure me? Isn't it worth a try?"

He looked like he wanted to pounce on me, but then furrowed his brow. "I don't want to hurt you."

"Maybe we could... go slow?" I pulled the sheet lower, letting the cotton slide down, revealing the curves of my body.

He groaned as he watched, his hands soon wandering where his eyes had traveled. His fingers grazed my sex, lightly playing over my folds as I gasped. Our lips met as he stroked me softly, his tongue sliding across my teeth.

"I don't usually do it like this," he said. "But right now, I just want to make you feel as good as possible."

I grinned, thinking of his dungeon. *No kidding.*

But I groaned as he leaned down and kissed his way around each breast, stopping to lap at each nipple until it tightened into a peak. I loved that he could be as tender as he was rough, drawing pleasure out of me the way a master musician draws beauty from his instrument.

When he entered me, it was slow and steady, his hips rocking forward and back, letting me adjust as we began our slow dance together. He looked into my eyes as we moved, the rhythm of his body matching each hitch of my breath, each small moan escaping from my lips.

When we came together, he kissed me, stealing my cries away, making me feel like we were part of one whole, one body, each part moving in perfect unison.

We lay together intertwined, tasting one another, touching and whispering, until the shriek of the hotel alarm clock brought our intimate moment to a halt.

It was the last day with the investors, after all.

We had work to do.

***

The morning activities were almost underway, but instead of facilitating, Mr. Drake wanted me to go back to the office ahead of him and gather the company's financial records from the last ten years. In secret and alone.

He gave me the master key to the CFO's office and sent me on my way with a look that sent chills down my spine. "These losses are not a coincidence, Isa. We have to find out what Lex did before he ruins this company. People are depending on us."

I nodded, my fists clenching by my sides. Could I do this? Sneak into the offices and get the documents while he distracted the investors?

As if he could read my mind, he said, "You're the only one who can help me. Now go."

So, I went.

The CFO's office wasn't as large as Mr. Drake's, but it felt vast as I fumbled for the light switch, the rows of filing cabinets rearing up as looming shadows against the curtain-covered windows. I found what we needed and began moving stacks of files onto my boss' desk, almost jumping out of my skin when the air conditioning switched on with a rumble. The building was, thankfully, empty, and I scurried from office to office without seeing another soul.

I made a pot of coffee and made a nest of files on the floor of my boss' office before getting down to business. At 5 p.m. I heard footsteps outside and tensed, my hands still full of photocopied receipts. The cadence of the steps became clear, and I relaxed. It was him. My Mr. Drake coming to help me at last.

Keys jingled and the heavy door swung inward.

"Isabeau."

My breath quickened at his outline in the doorway. He was wearing jeans and a soft, grey sweater that stretched neatly over his broad shoulders. It was something of a shock seeing him in anything but a suit or tuxedo, but my pulse pounding in my veins confirmed my thoughts. He was gorgeous, an air of elegance around him even in this relaxed state.

"Do you remember how I want you when we're in this office together?"

"Yes, Sir," I breathed.

I sat up on my knees and pushed them apart, putting my hands behind me. The slits of my skirt strained against my thighs as I assumed the position, and I cast my eyes down, even though all I wanted to do was meet that piercing green gaze.

"That's my good girl."

His voice was low, lustful, as he moved toward me. His shadow covered me, and I sighed, calmed by his presence, despite the coffee coursing through my veins.

"Have you found anything in the files?"

"Not yet, Sir," I said. "I've been going through the transaction records from the last quarter, but nothing's jumped out at me so far. The earnings figures are on your desk."

"Very good, little slave."

He wound his fingers in my hair and pulled, forcing me to look up into his eyes. "You've made your master very happy, Isa. Thank you for everything."

I blushed under his scrutiny, not expecting the

compliment when we were behaving... well, like *this*. The lines between work and play were blurring, and what's more was, I didn't mind.

He cupped my face with his other hand, caressing my cheek. His fingers traveled down my neck, making me tremble, before tracing the line of my collarbone. I didn't take my eyes off him while he held me like this, didn't want to even if he'd let me. His hand dipped lower, popping the top buttons of my blouse until I knew the swells of my breasts were exposed. He sucked in a sharp breath.

"Fuck." He broke eye contact, and I knew he was enjoying the view. "Stay right here, little slave. Close your eyes. Understood?"

"Yes, Sir."

I did as he asked, sitting back on my heels as I waited to see what he would do. There was the sound of the storage room door opening in the back of his office, then a scraping, like he was dragging something heavy over the carpet. There was a loud *thump*, then the sound of his footfalls returning.

"Open your eyes, Isa."

I opened them and was immediately more confused than enlightened. What was I looking at?

Sitting before me was a strange, and more than a little scary-looking, device, consisting of a black metal frame, wrist and ankle cuffs, and an ominous looking dildo-on-a-piston. *Oh, dear...*

Despite my hesitation, the thought of what Mr. Drake may want to do to me sent shivers of anticipation straight to my core.

"I want you." Mr. Drake's voice was hoarse with longing. "God, I always want you... But we need to figure out what's going on." He reached down and caressed my breasts through the silk, making me moan. "Lucky for us both, I do my best thinking when I'm sexually frustrated out of my mind."

He bent down and removed my diamond choker, replacing it with my black leather one. I smiled as he buckled it into place. The thought that he carried it with him was interesting, to say the least.

"Strip down, little slave, and get on all fours above the frame here."

I stood, slowly unbuttoning my blouse and unhooking my bra, loving the way he eyed me, his gaze all hunger and need. When my skirt and panties were folded on the floor next to me, I lowered myself down next to the cuffs, waiting for my next command. Mr. Drake knelt next to me and fastened me in, making sure I was comfortable, but secured in place. He lifted a bar off the frame, bringing it up under my chin. It had a padded rest in the shape of a U that he asked me to place my neck onto, and fastened the d-ring on my collar to the stockade.

I was completely trapped.

He moved behind me, and I tensed, a sudden jolt of fear stabbing through me as he adjusted the machine's piston arm. What would it feel like? Would it be too hard? Too fast?

I whimpered as I felt the black rubber of the dildo parting my folds.

"You're already so wet, little slave. So ready. I thought I'd have to lubricate it..."

I felt his hands slide over my cheeks, kneading the flesh. I groaned at his touch, wishing I could reach back and caress him, too. His lips brushed over me, and I squirmed against the restraints.

"You're absolutely amazing," he whispered.

His tongue darted out, tasting me.

"Now, I'm going to turn this on, and you're going to receive the fucking of a lifetime while I read these reports. When I've found what I'm looking for, I'll let you up again, and then take you myself. Understood?"

He stood and walked into view, sitting down at his desk. I stared, open mouthed before remembering myself.

"Y-yes, Sir..."

How long was he going to do this to me? What if I couldn't take it? What if he never found what he was looking for?

He hit a remote on his desk, his eyes flashing as he watched me. Before I could move, or even think, the dildo eased its way into me, stretching me around its girth. I gasped as it worked its way into my channel, my body squeezing around it as it filled me. Mr. Drake smiled.

"Good girl. Take it all in."

He pressed the buttons again, like he was turning up the volume on his television, and the machine began to whir, the piston warming up as it pulled out of me slowly, then pushed back in, making me bite my lip.

It was more than a little odd being shackled to this sex machine while Mr. Drake shuffled documents at his desk, stopping to stare at me once in a while and tap the controls, making the machine speed up, but if I was honest with myself, being helpless like this, letting him use me in such a domineering fashion right here in the office, was one of the most arousing things I'd ever experienced. It reminded me of being under his desk while he took that meeting, suckling him with my hands tied behind my back. I was his to control, and this little edge of danger, the thrilling fear of being caught, made it all the naughtier.

Mr. Drake came over, and knelt before me again, handing me a stack of receipts.

He grinned evilly as the machine pistoned into me back and forth again and again, my breasts swaying as I succumbed to its rhythm.

"You look beautiful like this, little slave. Your face so flushed and bright. Your body so pliant and eager. I want you to cum for me soon."

The bulge in his pants was just at mouth level. I longed for him to feed his length to me, to taste him as I knelt there, helpless and bound. Instead he moved back, leaving me with a file in each hand.

"Look these over, will you?"

I whined as the machine picked up speed, fucking me in a way that made my fists clench and my back arch beneath the onslaught. Mr. Drake laughed, the sound making the hairs on my neck stand on end. He was loving this, and the thought made me cry out, my body responding to his presence, his control... His desire.

I shuddered as I came, my lips forming his name as delicious heat spread through me, lighting up every nerve ending like stars in the night sky.

He was back at his desk when I came back down, my body overly sensitive and aching for more. His eyes burned into me, and I knew what he wanted. I awkwardly flipped open the files with each hand, cuffed as I was, and tried to focus on the papers within. My vision narrowed as the machine sped up again, pulsing as it drilled into me.

"Please!"

Mr. Drake just watched me, a wolfish grin plastered to his face.

"Get to work, Isabeau."

I looked down, moaning as the dildo passed in and out, rubbing my tender folds, the friction inside of me making my pleasure rise once again. I focused as best I could on the first receipt, my eyes blurring with tears. I didn't know if I could cum again, I was so sensitive, but I knew I was helpless to resist.

My eyes darted back to the stack of papers.

Cocktails at Morton's Pier Yacht Club. I twitched my fingers, shuffling the page to the side.

Golf at the Hayworth Greens. I moved it to look at the next.

Four cases of toner from Office Warehouse. Next receipt.

Coffee with clients. Next receipt.

Reams of paper. Next....

OH GOD...

All the words danced and swirled as my body contracted, the piston whirring in and out, faster and faster, electricity coursing through me until I couldn't stand it.

"Fuuuuck!"

I screamed as I came a second time, my thighs shaking as I convulsed again and again. Mr. Drake's eyes were scanning one of the earnings reports, but his lips twitched up into a smile at the sound of my cries.

"Please..."

I felt wrung out and too tender to even think about another orgasm. Every rasp of the black rubber against my lower lips sent jolts of sensation spiking through me, pleasure so intense it became pain. I was a raw nerve, exposed and delicate, being treated most *indelicately* by the heartless machine plowing into me as long as Mr. Drake saw fit to torture me like this.

I glanced down at the papers again, trying to distract myself from the pulsing inside the very heart of me, making my eyes water and my limbs tremble.

Dinner at the Morton's Pier Yacht Club.

Software license purchases.

Office supplies.

Gift cards for clients.

Edible arrangements.

Next, next, next...

I was at the very edge of my limits, and squeezed my eyes shut, trying to ward off the heightening spiral of overwhelming feeling so like pleasure, but as ruthlessly sharp as the edge of a knife, carrying me mercilessly toward another peak.

I cried then, tears running down my cheeks, wanting to pull away, but unable to budge. I didn't know if I could handle it if I came again. Maybe my atoms would fly apart, or my body would simply alight, the sensation burning me alive. Maybe I'd combust right here, setting his carpet on fire. Maybe, I'd... maybe...

All thought became impossible as I screamed again, wailing like a wounded animal as the orgasm took me, crashing over me with the force of a tsunami. In the distance, I heard Mr. Drake's voice, although the words had no meaning. Not while I was like this. Not while I was a slave to feeling, a human-sized nerve, and nothing more.

"I found it. Oh God, Isa, I found it here. He's taken it all. Everything."

The machine whirred to a stop, the dildo inching its way out of me with a wet *plop* that matched how I felt. Like a puddle, poured out over the restraints, a spill on the office floor instead of Isabeau.

Strong hands unhooked the restraints and pulled me gently to my feet. I leaned on Mr. Drake, unable to stand just yet.

"Oh, my sweet Isabeau. I wish I could linger in this moment with you, but we can't. I need you to come back to me, little slave. Come back and get dressed. I need your help. Now, more than ever."

He held me tight for a moment, supporting me and rubbing my back, letting me come back to being myself again. When I could finally stand, his words caught up to me.

"What do you mean 'he's taken it all?' Lex is just outright embezzling?"

"He was, but it's worse than that. The pension fund is completely cleaned out. He must have been planning this for ages, but... I just hope we're not too late to stop him. The employees' retirement fund..."

I slipped my underwear on as quickly as I could, and reached for my skirt. "We need to call the police."

"We have to find him *now*, Isa. He must have planned his withdrawals to coincide with the investor weekend, so I wouldn't be watching the accounts. If he made a move like this, then he's probably trying to leave the country. Today, if he can."

I slipped on my bra and shoved my arms through the sleeves of my blouse. "We need to call the airports. Tell them to be on the lookout for him, and then call the police." I looked around for my heels. Mr. Drake handed them to me.

"I'll drive. You call." He handed me his cell phone and grabbed the file he'd been examining.

We were jogging out of his office toward the elevator bank when a thought hit me.

"What if he knew we'd be in the office today? Especially after your fight last night, he must know you'd be suspicious of him."

He stabbed at the elevator button, his posture rigid. His hand drummed impatiently against his leg. "What does it matter if he knew we'd be here?"

"If he thought ahead, he would know we'd call the airlines and the authorities first thing, to try to trap him. He has to leave the country to retrieve the money, right?"

Mr. Drake's jaw tightened. "Yes. He would have wired it into an offshore account."

"Then what if he's not going to the airport? What if he has another way to leave?"

The elevator pinged and we stepped inside. Mr. Drake's face was unreadable. "What are you thinking, Isabeau?"

The receipts I'd be staring at while I was shackled tugged at the edge of my mind.

"Does Lex own a yacht, by chance?"

Mr. Drake ran a hand over his face. "*Shit.* He does, but I don't know where he keeps it. I've never been on it."

"He's been spending a lot of time at the Morton's Pier Yacht Club. There are several receipts for cocktails and dinners there just from the last month."

Mr. Drake's face broke into a grin that lit up the elevator. "Isabeau... you never cease to amaze me. I could kiss you right now."

"Only if you can manage it before we get to the garage!" We'd be in cell range then, with no more time to waste, even for something as sweet as that.

He crushed me to him, kissing me hard and deep, pouring out his thanks in a way that made my heart feel like it was going to pound out of my chest.

The elevator doors slid open, and we broke apart.

"Let's go," he said. "I just pray we get to him in time."

9 AT HIS SIDE

I dialed the police, then listened to the ringing on the other end, harmonizing with the squealing tires of Mr. Drake's car as he rocketed out of the parking lot toward Morton's Pier. I pulled on the edge of my skirt, my hands restless as I waited for someone to pick up the phone. Mr. Drake's jaw was set, his eyes glued to the road. Finally, there was a click on the other end of the line. I spoke before the operator could finish his greeting.

"Yes, hello? Please, we need to report a crime. It's an emergency."

I tried to keep my voice calm even while adrenaline coursed through me at the thought that all those people--people I'd had lunch with, sat with during meetings, chatted with in the break room--could lose everything if we didn't stop Lex in time.

Mr. Drake's knuckles were white against the steering wheel as he cut through traffic. I gave as many details as I could to the operator, telling them to send squad cars to look for Alexander Smith at the airport, but that we suspected he was trying to flee the country by sea.

"Please, stay on the line, Ms. Willcox," the operator said. "We're sending squad cars to meet you at the pier. Don't make a move until we get there."

"No problem."

I held the phone to my ear, my hand now slippery with sweat. The car jumped as Mr. Drake crashed over a speed bump, roaring into the outer parking lot of the marina. The gate was down, the striped barrier arm down over entrance to the Yacht Club, blocking access. Mr. Drake swore beside me, before slamming the car to a halt. Without another word, he jerked the keys out of the ignition and barreled out of the car, slamming the door behind him.

"They said to wait!" I called, but he was already gone, running down the pier. "Shit."

"What's that, Ma'am?" The operator's voice in my ear startled me.

"Please hurry," I said, and ended the call.

I jumped out of the car and went after Mr. Drake, ducking low under the barrier, grateful once again for the hidden slits in my skirt that allowed such movement, although I doubt they were ever intended for crime fighting.

I crossed the parking lot, my heels clicking loudly on the pavement as I broke into a jog. Mr. Drake disappeared around the north side of the huge building sprawling before me, blocking the view of the dock. I hurried after, hoping to catch up to him, when I caught something moving in the corner of my vision.

A pink blur registered, and I turned just in time to see a petite blonde with a rolling suitcase disappear around the south side. She hadn't seen me, but the brief glimpse I'd gotten of her was hauntingly familiar. I changed direction, edging closer to the edge of the building, moving more slowly now so the sound of my heels wouldn't give me away. I peered around the corner and stifled a gasp.

Veronica, or as Lex had dubbed her, The Future Mrs. Drake, was sashaying ahead of me, her Chanel purse full to bursting, a curling iron cord dangling from the open zipper, dragging her suitcase behind her. Where was *she* going in such a hurry?

This was too much of a coincidence. If she was here,

now, packed for a journey, she might lead me straight to Lex. I trotted along behind her, hiding in the shadows of the doorways as we made our way past the main club building and toward the smaller outbuildings behind it.

When we moved toward a large boathouse at the edge of the dock, I glanced around us. Where was Mr. Drake? I thought I'd find him around back, but he was nowhere to be seen. As I edged around the boathouse, I saw them--row after row of large, white yachts floating quietly in the harbor, moored side by side like sleeping giants.

Veronica was disappearing down the wood planking, taking a turn and disappearing behind the bulk of the first row of vessels. I followed, hoping my hunch was correct, and I'd be able to lead the police straight to Lex when they arrived.

I slowed down when I reached the corner Veronica's swaying pink purse had just disappeared around. The sound of male voices reached my ears, and I peered around the hull of *The Ex-Wife*, hoping to remain unseen in the shadow of the yacht.

"You don't have to do this, Lex. This is between you and me. Let's talk this through before you do something you'll regret."

"Don't flatter yourself, Chase! This is about *me* getting what I deserve. Living in your shadow should guarantee me a fucking bonus, after all the shit I've put up with over the years."

"The employees are the ones who will suffer, and you know it. If you want to get back at me, take anything else. Just not the pensions. Even *you* aren't that selfish, Lex."

"Did you ever think maybe it's not just about the cash? Maybe I want to relish the thought of all those people knowing that you let them down. Of you tossing and turning at night as you wondered how you didn't see it coming. The guilt of your failure eating you alive. Maybe that's the only thing I want as I sail away to a brand new life."

I saw Mr. Drake now. His back was to me on the dock in

front of Lex, who was standing on the ladder on the side of his yacht, ready to board. They hadn't seen Veronica yet. She was lurking in the shadows by a pile of rope, digging in her purse, her suitcase forgotten at her feet.

Where the hell are the cops already? My ears strained for the sound of sirens, but the seconds ticked by, and we were still all alone.

"Please, Lex... I'll go away if you'd like. Leave the city. We can pretend this never happened, and I'll leave the company quietly. Just come down from there and talk to me."

Mr. Drake moved toward the yacht, his hand outstretched, urging Lex to come with him.

"Freeze, Chasey!"

Both men's eyes shot wide as Veronica's shrill voice rang out over the water. She held a revolver in her perfectly manicured hands, the barrel pointed straight at Mr. Drake's chest.

"One more move, and I'll shoot, Mister! Back away nice and slow."

"Nice work, Ronnie," Lex said, grinning in a way that made my blood boil. "You've got great timing."

He hopped down off the ladder and stood in front of Mr. Drake, his hands on his hips. Veronica advanced on him, gun held steady, the light of the setting sun glinting off the weapon.

"You were right, Lexy. I'm glad I took daddy's gun like you said."

"Search him," Lex said. "Make sure he doesn't have his cell phone. We don't want him to try anything funny when we leave him tied up. We want to be well on our way by the time anyone knows we're gone.."

Mr. Drake's face was dark, his forehead furrowed as Veronica moved toward him.

This had gone far enough. They were going to get away if I didn't act fast.

I flicked the phone open and dialed the last number, leaving it ringing silently on the wooden boards of the dock. I stumbled around the corner like I'd been running, my chest heaving dramatically.

"Wait!"

All eyes landed on me, Veronica's gun barrel twitching as she tried to decide whether to cover me or Chase Drake.

"Take me with you, Lex," I said, moving closer, raising my hands in the air. "You were right about me. I only wanted Chase when I thought he was the powerhouse behind the business. The successful one." I breathed heavily, holding a stitch in my side. "I want to come along..."

"Stay right there, bitch!" Veronica's hands shook as she trained the gun on me.

Something in my chest tightened in reaction to staring down the barrel of a real-life gun, but I steadied my emotions.

Keep going, Isabeau. You can do this. You have to!

Chase Drake needed me to keep a cool head, and that was exactly what I was going to do.

I stopped, but trained my eyes on Lex. He looked incredulous, but ran a hand over his chin, looking me up and down in a way that made my skin crawl.

"I was always attracted to you, but..." I looked guiltily at Mr. Drake. "I didn't want to ruin my chances with him while I had a good thing going. Please, Lex. Take me with you. We can be together now. Now that I know who the real man is."

"What?!" Veronica's pink lips were pulled back in a snarl. "First you take my Chasey and now you're making a play for him?" She turned to Lex, her barrel drifting away from my chest. "Tell her to go to hell, baby!"

But Lex had a twinkle in his black eyes like all of his Christmases were coming early, and I knew I had him.

"I want you, Lex," I said, my voice breathy and high. "Please. You know how much fun we can have together. It'll be so good..."

I stepped closer, and Veronica practically bristled as she looked back and forth between me and the man she'd planned to run away with. She turned the barrel on him, and his eyes widened.

"Tell her, Lexy! *Tell her!*"

He reached toward her, his eyes pleading. "C'mon, baby. Lower the gun. Don't be hysterical."

"Hysterical?!" Veronica's face reddened and she ground her high heel into the dock. "You tell me I'm all you ever wanted, that you can love me better than Chasey ever could, and now you're seriously considering letting this gutter-trash-slut come with us?"

"Baby, it's not like that..."

"THEN WHAT'S IT LIKE?"

Lex's gaze shifted, and I could tell he was trying to think of something, anything, to get him out of hot water and onto his yacht before things could get any worse. And that was why neither he nor Veronica saw Mr. Drake lunge for the gun.

It all happened so fast, that if I had blinked, I would have missed it. Chase Drake's hand closed around the barrel, twisting it out of Veronica's fingers. She screamed bloody murder, and Lex tried to scrabble up the ladder of his boat when Mr. Drake shouted.

"Hold it right there! Drop to the dock, Lex!"

Veronica raised her claws like she was planning to scratch Chase's face off, and that's when I leapt into action, tackling her onto the dock. She thrashed in my grip, and I crushed her into the planks.

The wood thudded beneath me, and suddenly I realized it was the impact of several pairs of boots approaching at a run.

"Police! Smith, get down on the ground!"

Officers in blue surrounded us, guns drawn. I raised my head just in time to see Lex Smith getting dragged off his ladder like a kitten out of a tree, and grinned.

Veronica had frozen beneath my body, and now a police officer held a hand out to me. I gripped it and let her pull me to my feet, smiling all the while as she cuffed Veronica and recited her Miranda rights.

I looked over at Mr. Drake and saw him looking back at

me, his face glowing with pride.

We'd really done it. The employee pensions were safe, and so were we.

"You'll never be anything but trash, Isabeau," Lex yelled as two police officers gripped his arms. "You're nothing! You hear me?"

"Wait a second," I said to the officers, and they paused, holding Lex still.

I walked up to him and leaned in close to whisper in his ear. "It must be hard, being such a small, small man, living in the shadow of a giant."

My knee shot out before the police could stop me, nailing him right in the balls. He wheezed, his eyes filling with tears.

"Who knows? Maybe you'll be the number one scumbag on your cell block. There's always something to hope for, Lex. Keep your head up."

I heard one of the officers snicker as I walked away, my eyes locked on Chase Drake.

It was finally over.

***

I sat wrapped in a thick blanket on Mr. Drake's leather sofa, snuggled up next to a roaring fire. He poured me a cup of brandy and handed it to me, the firelight playing over his strong jaw and wavy hair, making me want to reach up and trace the lines of his face, to run my fingertips over his lips. Instead, I sipped the golden liquid, sighing as its warmth spread through me.

"I couldn't have done it without you, Isabeau."

His voice was barely over a whisper, a low rumble that filled my senses, causing my tension to melt away like the fragments of a dream.

"Good thing you didn't have to," I said, grinning up at him.

Maybe it was the sip of spirits, or maybe it was just the

relief after a suspense-filled day, but I felt almost giddy, there with him, safe and sound in a mansion I was slowly getting comfortable in.

"I mean it, Isa." He took my glass and set it aside, then captured my hands in his. "The police wouldn't have found us in time if the cell phone signal hadn't led them right to us." He paused, kissing my fingers. "You're just amazing."

I looked down at our hands intertwined, at his long fingers holding mine, his touch making me tingle from head to toe.

"I could say the same about you. The way you took the gun from Veronica. Hell, just the way you discovered what he was up to in the first place."

His face darkened. "I should have seen it sooner. The employees deserve better."

"You are their hero, today."

He paused, staring at me with those green eyes that made my knees turn to jelly.

"Isa... I have something to ask you, and I'm not quite sure how to start. Please... close your eyes."

The twinge of anxiety in his voice made the hair on the back of my neck stand on end. What was going on? Why would cause my strong, dominant Mr. Drake to be afraid after a day like this?

I closed my eyes and waited for what was to come, feeling the warmth of the fire on my face. I let the blanket fall to my sides and knotted my hands together, worrying, despite the feeling of safety I'd just enjoyed.

There was a rustling, then Mr. Drake's hand covered mine once again.

"Open them, Isabeau."

I opened my eyes and gasped. Tears sprung to my eyes as I saw my master, my love, kneeling before me, his green gaze piercing me. A ring glinted in his other hand, a cluster of diamonds forming a blossom in the middle of a beautifully carved platinum band.

"Isa, I'm sorry I couldn't wait to do more... to make this

moment perfect... because you deserve that and so much more. But I couldn't spend another moment with you without asking you this."

I trembled, my whole body shaking as I gripped his hand in mine, not daring to move, or even speak, lest I discover I was dreaming. That this wasn't really happening, and Chase Drake wasn't on his knees before me.

"Since I met you, my life has been different than I ever thought it could be. I never imagined I'd find someone who I could trust so completely, not only with my secrets, but with my heart. I didn't know anyone could be my perfect match. Isa..." He held the ring up to me, his eyes full of need. "Will you be my partner? My wife? Will you say yes and make my life what I always wanted, but never dreamed possible?"

For a moment, my breath caught in my chest. Time stood still, and it was just me and him, looking into one another's eyes and envisioning eternity together. Working together, living together, loving one another as only we could.

Without a word, I slid off the couch and wrapped my arms around him, bringing my lips to his. We fit together like two pieces of a puzzle, his mouth opening to me as I deepened the kiss, pouring out all of my love and hope and promise into that one moment. Salt flavored our lips, and I realized tears were rolling down my cheeks, flowing freely at the thought of being his wife.

I pulled back, smiling even as I swiped at the wetness on my cheeks.

"Yes, Sir," I said.

He laughed, pulling me back into his arms, holding me on his lap in front of the fire.

"This ring was my grandmother's," he said, his breath tickling my ear as he held me tightly to him. "I didn't have time to buy one for you, but I will. You'll have whatever you desire, my beautiful Isa."

I broke away and held out my left hand, urging him to place it on my finger. "It's perfect. It couldn't be more perfect if I'd picked it out myself."

He slid the ring onto my finger, my skin coming alive beneath the cool metal band.

"I love that it was in your family. One day, maybe I can pass it on to our child."

He stared at me for a moment in silence, assessing me, then broke into a smile that made my heart ache.

"I've never met a woman like you."

It was my turn to smile. "I've never met a man like you, either."

He pulled me down with him, laying me back on the soft rug before the roaring fire. "Then I guess we're lucky we found one another."

He leaned over, pressing into me, his erection hitting me in just the right spot to make me moan. I spread my legs, wrapping them around him, holding him to me as his lips captured mine once again.

I was going to marry Chase Drake. The wish I didn't know I'd had was coming true, and in that moment, I knew-- things would never be the same.

***

Three months later...

I screeched as Mr. Drake scooped me off my feet, the white fabric of my wedding dress swirling around his crisp tuxedo shirt. He tossed me over his shoulder and opened the hidden door to his dungeon. He swatted my backside, making me giggle.

"What kind of husband would I be if I didn't carry you over the threshold?"

I grinned against his back, my hair spilling out of my chignon. He kicked the door closed behind us and set me down. He pulled me into a kiss that made my head spin, holding me tightly in his strong arms. When he pulled away, his eyes were blazing.

149

I still couldn't believe I was married to this man, my love, my Mr. Drake.

"I don't have a gift for you," I said. "I didn't know I was supposed to... and after what you gave me, I don't know what I could do for you that would even compare."

"Isa." He wound his fingers in my hair, toying with the curls now falling down around my shoulders. "Making you partner in the business wasn't a wedding gift, you silly girl. I just wanted to surprise you today to make it even more special. You will accept, won't you?"

I looked down at my shoes, searching for the right words. The dim light of the dungeon made the antique ring seem to glow on my hand, the diamond flashing as I fidgeted. I glanced back up, suddenly shy.

"Well, we *do* make a great team."

His lips twitched into a lopsided grin. "And your name *is* already on the building. *Mrs*. Drake."

The words sounded so sweet, so right, that I wondered how I'd ever been called anything else.

"Then that's settled," I said, biting my lip. "If you want me, Mr. Drake, I'm yours."

Mr. Drake's eyes caught mine, the hunger in them taking my breath away. He looked me over, his gaze sliding down over the slinky white silk of my wedding gown, and for a moment, he looked like a panther ready to pounce.

"God, yes," he growled. "I've never wanted you more."

He reached forward, his strong fingers shooting toward my straps, ready to tear my gown off my shoulders.

"Wait!" I yelled. "Not this dress!"

He stopped short and grinned, then moved behind me and started slowly unbuttoning the long line of pearl buttons down my back. His slow, methodical movements were driving me crazy. I longed to be in his arms, and wondered if he was going extra slowly just to torture me. I tapped my foot impatiently, and heard his low laugh against my ear. When the last button was undone, he pushed the straps gently over my shoulders and let the gown slither to the floor. I stepped out of it and heard him draw a shuddering breath.

I smiled over my shoulder at him, delighting in the appreciation in his eyes. I wore nothing but a white lace garter belt beneath my dress, delicate bows clasping the tops of my sheer, ivory stockings, caressing my legs all the way down to my high heels. I turned around, then knelt on the ground before him, spreading my thighs and placing my hands behind my back until my breasts jutted forward. My nipples drew into peaks under his gaze, ready and eager for his touch.

"Good girl, Isa," he said, looking down at me. "I have one last surprise for you before I make you mine, once and for all."

I waited, my heart racing as he retrieved a black, lacquered box from one of the dungeon's shelves. He knelt before me and opened it up.

"Put it on, little slave. It's yours."

My hands trembled as I picked up the leather collar. Unlike my other one, this was as white as snow, the buckle gleaming like the ring on my finger. The leather was soft, caressing my skin as I fastened it on, feeling instantly like a part of me. Like it belonged there, just like I belonged here. With him.

"Beautiful," he said, his long fingers stroking my face. "Just beautiful."

"Thank you, Sir," I breathed.

"Come here, Isa. Come to the cross."

He beckoned for me to stand and follow him to the back of the dungeon, where the enormous X-shaped cross stood against the wall. I trembled looking at it, adrenaline coursing through my body at the thought of being bound to it, spread wide and helpless before my master.

"I know you've been waiting for this. The way you looked at it the first day I brought you down here... I've been saving it for you. For the perfect moment."

I tried to steady my breathing as I stared up at it, then down at the black nylon rope lying in a neat coil at its base.

"Put your back against it, little slave. Hold your arms out."

I did as he commanded, holding my arms in place as he deftly wound the rope through a ring at the top of each arm of the cross, then secured my wrists to the polished wood. Once each of my arms were secure, he wound the rope in an intricate pattern, binding it over the tops of my breasts, then under, displaying them proudly, before snaking the rope back and forth like a web around my waist and thighs. I spread my legs for him, and he bound those, too, lashing me securely to the cross.

He leaned back, studying his work, his long fingers running over his chin. He smiled, then, and untied his tie, then slowly unbuttoned his crisp, white shirt. I licked my lips as he revealed the strong planes of his chest, wishing I could run my hands through the sprinkling of golden brown hair, then move lower, tracing the lines of his contoured abs until I reached the place just above his belt, tickling the flesh above the place I wanted to touch most of all.

He was naked now from the waist up, and grinning at me in a way that sent shivers down my spine. I tried my bonds, but I was snugly held, the rope rubbing against my wrists when I tried to move.

He stepped into the shadows and returned with another box, one I remembered all too well. He opened the lid, and I sucked in a breath--the egg and the plug he'd made me wear before where there, along with a small vial of lubricant.

He wasn't going to use those on me, was he? All I wanted was him inside of me, filling me up, making me truly his wife, his partner, his love.

"Relax, little slave," he said, his voice a low rumble in the dimness. "Trust your master."

I relaxed against the wood of the cross, my body humming in anticipation. He came to me, looming over me, and I gasped when I felt cool gel hit my pucker.

"Shhh, Isa. Take it in," he whispered, and pressed the thin plug into me.

I breathed out, accepting it, and it slipped inside, the feel of it stretching my tight ring of muscle making me whimper.

Mr. Drake slipped a hand into his pocket, and the egg whirred to life, buzzing against the wood of the box. He swept it up and held it before my eyes, letting me wonder what exactly he was going to do with it.

"Remember this, little girl? How you came around it, shuddering in my arms as we danced? How raw you were, Isa... How *real*. It was breathtaking."

He brought the egg to my lips, and I opened my mouth, suckling on it gently.

"I knew then, you were someone very special. Someone I couldn't let get away."

The buzzing egg lowered, and I moaned as he ran it over one nipple, making it tighten to a peak, then the other, the coolness from my mouth making the vibration feel even more powerful against my hot flesh. He trailed the egg around the curve of my breasts, trussed up by his skillful rope work, making me tremble as it glided over me.

I was already wet for him, my body squeezing around the plug, arousal leaking down onto my thighs. How I wanted him in me... but he seemed determined to tease me. To drive me wild before finally giving me what I wanted. What I needed.

He moved the egg lower, tracing the gentle curves of my body, bringing the vibration against the sensitive flesh on my inner thigh, making me squeal and pull at the ropes. His chuckle made my body tingle, aching for him, but helpless to take him into my arms. When the egg hit my delicate folds, I cried out, my muscles squeezing around the plug, pleasure spiking through me like lightning. He moved it in circles, grinding it against my clit until I was gasping, tears stinging my eyes.

Mr. Drake reached into his pocket again, and the plug inside of me roared to life, matching the vibrations from the egg. I was enfolded in feeling, my entire lower half pulsing, my head spinning as I felt the orgasm already building inside of me, coiling deep in my belly.

He bent down, and I wailed as he nibbled my breasts,

rubbing the egg harder against me as his teeth found their way to my nipples, already painfully erect.

With one swift movement, he pushed the egg between my legs, pressing it up inside of me. I screamed as he latched onto one nipple, biting hard, his tongue thrashing over the tip as the sweet pain made my body shake against my restraints. The throbbing inside of me reached a crescendo, and then I was cumming, crying out his name as a hot tear rolled down my cheek.

His mouth gentled on me, kissing and sucking, and he moved to the other breast as my body trembled, convulsing around the toys still humming inside of me. Then, the vibrations stopped, and he was lowering his pants and boxers to the floor.

"Push it out now, little slave."

I panted against my restraints, but did as I was told, squeezing my muscles until the egg was released into my master's hand.

"Good girl."

His breath tickled my ear before his lips trailed down my neck, kissing and licking.

I mewled, wanting him, wanting more, but not sure how much more I could take. He moved closer, his hard chest brushing against my breasts. I loved the way he felt against me--so safe, so warm. So *right*.

He reached down, and I felt the tip of him pressing into me, urging me open. I moaned as he sheathed himself inside of me, stretching me; filling me in a way that made my toes curl inside of my heels. I was spread wide for him, vulnerable and ready, and he pushed deeper, making me gasp.

"Is this what you want, Mrs. Drake?" He grabbed my waist, pulling out in one achingly slow motion, before slamming home once again. "Is this what you want from me?"

"Yes," I moaned. "Yes, Sir!"

He leaned in, capturing my mouth in a long, sensual kiss, his tongue mimicking the movement of his hips as he thrust into me again, pulled out, then thrust back even harder. I groaned at the feel of him, each long stroke of his cock inside of me making my sensitive body rejoice. When he broke away, he bit my earlobe, making me cry out.

"You're mine, Isabeau. All mine," he said, grunting as he drove into me.

"Yes," I breathed. "God, yes, Mr. Drake."

He picked up his pace, and I could tell he was at the edge of his control--that he wanted me just as badly as I wanted him, and this time couldn't restrain himself, couldn't take his sweet time torturing me, drawing it out. The thought made my heat sear through me, the intensity of his lovemaking, his lust, making me burn for him. He reached down, and suddenly, the plug buzzed to life again, making me scream, the pressure rubbing against the friction of his shaft inside of me.

"And I'm yours, Isa. All yours. For as long as I live..."

Tears rolled down my cheeks again, but not just from the pleasure threatening to overwhelm my every sense. I was his, and he was mine. Husband and wife. For the rest of our lives...

He drove into me, kissing my tears away as he fucked me ravenously, drawing out, then driving home again and again, over and over. I strained against the ropes, wanting to cry out, but unable to speak, as I exploded against the hard wood of the cross.

He groaned and kissed me, locking us together as he came along with me, our bodies convulsing as one, intertwined, locked together in passion. In love.

When we finally stilled, he held my face in his hands, the look in his eyes echoing everything welling up inside my own heart. When he said, "I love you, Isabeau," I nodded. It wasn't necessary. I was Mrs. Drake, his and only his, and I knew I was loved.

And in that moment, I knew I was home as well.

~The End~

If you enjoyed falling in love along with Chase and Isabeau, stay tuned for exciting new erotic romance releases from Delilah Fawkes!

Delilah loves hearing from her readers on her blog at http://www.delilahfawkes.blogspot.com, or by email at delilahfawkes@gmail.com. Please sign up for her mailing list on her blog to keep up with new releases and special deals just for subscribers.

Reviews are also a huge help to independent authors, so if you enjoyed this story, please consider reviewing it at Amazon.com. Thank you so much for reading!

Keep reading for a BONUS story, just for you...

MY BEST FRIEND'S BROTHER

I took the bottle of spiced rum from Savannah's limp hand. She'd definitely had enough, and was sleeping like the dead, sprawled out on the foot of Amber's bed. These two were serious lightweights.

I pressed my freshly glossed lips to the bottle, and took a long swig. It was ridiculous that these two were asleep already, ruining the slumber party we'd planned. I mean, it was only 2 a.m.! We hadn't even watched any Skin-imax movies yet, for God's sakes, and had just barely started gossiping when they passed out.

I washed down the rum with the swig of cola, and got up. If these two were going to be party poopers, I would make my own fun. Amber's folks were vacationing in Europe, so I had free reign of the house. *I bet they have a stack of really screwed up pornos somewhere.* Rich people always did.

I padded barefoot out to the living room in my white panties and tank top, my firm breasts braless—just the way I liked them. I searched in the usual places. Behind the big screen. In the back of the liquor cabinet, and finally in the desk drawer in the den.

Bingo. I pulled the DVD out and stared at the bare ass on the cover.

"Barely Legal Butt Fucking? Huh." I never fancied

Amber's dad for an ass man, especially not the way he'd always stared at my tits whenever I came over. Go figure.

I heard a noise from down the hallway like a sigh. Were the girls awake again? Could we rekindle this party after all? I put the DVD back in the drawer and moved into the hallway, tiptoeing toward the sound. I paused outside Amber's room. A rattling snore met my ears that sounded like Savannah's.

Classy.

Then, I heard it. A muffled groan, coming from a room three doors down. Amber's brother's room. I'd forgotten that Brian was back from college this weekend. He'd been quiet all evening, and I wondered if he'd been in his room the whole time.

I leaned closer, straining to hear better.

"Oh, yeah, baby..." A rough whisper carried through the thin wood of the door. "Take my cock just like that."

I covered my hand with my mouth to hold back my giggle. He was totally touching himself in there! I pictured Brian—tall, fit from his years on the swim team, with gorgeous green eyes and messy black hair—lying back on his bed, fisting his dick. The thought made my mouth water. I'd always had a thing for him throughout high school. Hell, he was half the reason I hung out with Amber in the first place.

"Yeah..." he whispered again, and I pressed my ear to the door. "Fuck me, Bailey."

My pussy clenched at the mention of my name. He was thinking about *me*... about my tight cunt riding him. Or maybe taking me from behind. God, it couldn't be! It was just too good. Brian Sanders was fantasizing about *me* while he jerked off.

"Take it all. Don't make me spank you, bitch... yeah..."

I almost groaned out in the hallway, but kept my mouth shut. I loved the idea of his large hand slapping my firm ass as he fucked me.

"You're a greedy little slut aren't you? Yeah, Bailey..."

I could hear the slap of skin on skin.

I *was* a greedy little slut. A self-proclaimed nympho, I was well-known as a lover of the cock, and right now was no exception. My pussy was getting so wet listening to Brian touch himself. I wanted to come. *Needed* to. I squeezed my thighs together, shooting a tingle through my clit.

Before I could talk myself out of it, I eased the door open and slipped into his room. Brian's eyes were closed as he slid his hand up and down his rock hard cock. He hadn't heard me come in, but still lay on his bedspread, naked, touching himself.

I'll admit it. I stared.

His cock was one of the thickest I'd ever seen, and I couldn't help wondering how it would feel inside my tight little pussy. Would it hurt? Or would it feel just right?

"Bailey," he groaned, his hips bucking up to meet his fist.

I peeled off my tank top and threw it across the room, nailing him in the face with it.

"Yes, Brian?"

He yelped and whipped the tank off his face, his eyes wide. He then used it to cover his junk.

"Wh-what? Oh, God! Bailey?"

His eyes locked on my round breasts, then traveled down to my panties. My nipples hardened beneath his gaze.

"Did I hear you talking about me, Brian, while you rubbed that big dick of yours?"

I smiled coyly. I loved the way flashes of panic mixed with the arousal on his flushed face.

"Uh… oh, geez, Bailey. I… I didn't know you could hear me." He ran a hand through his black hair, making it stand on end.

He was so adorably sexy. I knew he just wanted to melt into the floor and die.

"I'm glad I did."

I moved to sit on his bed, my breasts bobbing as I walked. His eyes followed the motion—they were practically glued to my chest. I sat next to him and leaned close. I could smell the light scent of his pine deodorant, mixing with the musky smell of the pre-cum I knew was beading on that cock of his, hidden beneath my tank top.

"You are?" His voice was husky, and his eyes darkened as he met my gaze.

"Mmm hmm. I've always wanted to fuck you, Brian." I straddled his legs, pushing him back onto his pillows. His eyes shot wide.

"Oh... God..."

"And now that your sissy and her friend are asleep, I can screw your brains out without her knowing." I grinned wickedly, and brushed my breasts over his naked chest, dragging my nipples across his hot skin.

He made a strangled sound, and I felt his cock rise up to brush my thigh. I snatched the tank top away and gently rubbed my wet panties against the head, letting him feel how aroused I was.

"Unless, of course, you don't want me to fuck you."

I tilted my head to one side, waiting for his answer. I wanted him so badly. I hoped he wouldn't chicken out on me.

"I want you," he gasped.

His arms encircled my waist, and he pulled me down to him, kissing me hard. I was caught off guard by his aggression, but melted into him as his tongue met mine. He was an amazing kisser. It was like his tongue had a life of its own inside my mouth; prodding, teasing, sucking. I sighed into him, and felt my nipples pucker further against his hard chest. One of his hands snaked into my hair, while the other grabbed my ass, roughly pulling me closer.

Without warning, his hand came down on my ass cheek with a *smack*. I screeched, and he pulled my hair, lifting my face to his.

"If you want this, you're going to do it my way," he breathed.

Oh, God. I'd never seen this side of him. Was he seriously trying to dominate me in the sack?

My mouth was hanging open, and I closed it with a snap.

"What? Ahh!"

His hand came down again, stinging my cheek as I straddled him. The glow on my backside turned into a sharp pleasure, making my pussy even wetter. I'd always wanted to be spanked, but I never saw a stand up guy like Brian being the one to do it.

"You heard me, you slut. You do what I say, or you get out of my bedroom."

His hand cupped my breast, then he pinched my nipple. *Hard.*

I should have been pissed off. I should have left. I should have punched him in the dick. No one told *me* what to do. I was always the seductor—always in charge. But, I had to admit... having a boy take control like this was a rush. Was he man enough to rein me in?

"I'll do what you say, Brian."

I licked my lips, and he released my hair.

"Good."

He pulled me into another mind-blowing kiss, his tongue rasping across my teeth. I couldn't breath, but I didn't care. He could kiss me senseless like that all night long. He let me go too soon.

"Give me those tits, Bailey."

He pulled me higher, so my breasts were level with his mouth, then pressed them together, so my nipples pointed straight at him.

He groaned. "You're so beautiful."

His tongue darted out, licking first one nipple than the next, flicking them softly. I moaned and gripped his shoulders. His cock nestled in the crack of my ass, twitching as he licked me. God, it was so erotic.

He suckled my nipples one at a time, sending jolts all the way down my body. His teeth scraped over one before drawing on it greedily. I squirmed against him, wanting more, wanting everything.

"Panties off. I want to taste that sweet little cunt of yours."

I gasped at his words. Brian was quite the surprise. Not your usual pump-chump jock at all. I stood, giving me an eyeful of the wet spot on my panties, then lowered them and stepped out of the pair, kicking them off the bed with one foot.

"Sit on my face, baby. I want to taste you coming all over my tongue."

I groaned, then lowered down until my knees were on either side of his head. I'd never ridden a guy's face before. They were usually so much more selfish, and I usually jumped right on their cock, because, let's face it: I was, too. I wanted what I wanted, and I wanted it *now*.

I lowered my soaking pussy over his lips nervously, but he grabbed my ass cheeks and forced me down, clamping his mouth around my folds. I gripped the top of the headboard for balance, and was immediately glad I did. At that moment, his tongue began swirling over my lower lips, running back and forth, dipping into my hole, then circling my clit. The onslaught was like nothing I'd ever felt.

I threw my head back and moaned. He suckled hard on my clit, then began the circling motion again, working my pussy for all he was worth. My abs tightened as pleasure built up inside me, coiling though my body. Just when I was right on the edge, he pulled back, licking gently at my entrance, but avoiding my clit.

I grunted in frustration, but his hand smacked my bottom again, over and over. I screeched and tried to escape his iron grip.

He came up for air. "Do you know my nickname, Bailey?" His face was glistening with my juices, and he licked his lips greedily.

"Yeah. Hurricane."

"You know why they call me that?"

I'd actually thought it was some swim team thing, or a move he did in the water, but now I wasn't so sure.

"They call me that because I'm the best at what I do. I fucking love licking a wet cunt, Bailey, and I know exactly how to swirl and blow, and at the end, you'll be totally destroyed. I'm a hurricane, baby."

I sighed and my thighs clenched next to his head with anticipation.

"Now, I'm going back in. Hold on, baby."

He pulled me back down onto him and began again, circling his tongue in a calculated frenzy, sucking at the right times, then jamming his entire tongue into my hole, fucking me with his face. He brought me right to the crest again and again, always pulling back when he sensed I was close and my legs started shaking.

When I thought I couldn't take it anymore, he clamped down on my clit and sucked for all he was worth. My pleasure ratcheted up to an almost painful level, and I squirmed, either trying to get away, or trying to give him better access—I didn't know, and I didn't care. My mind was being wiped clean, and all I could feel was his tongue, his lips, his teeth-- licking and rasping and sucking. My whole world had narrowed to the feeling overtaking me, burning inside my very core.

He bit down on my clit, and I came undone, bucking wildly on his face, squeezing him with my thighs. The orgasm was too intense, too good. He'd built it up with his careful assault, pulling back, then charging, until I was coming so hard, my vision was fading. All that existed was my throbbing, pulsing, clenching pussy, creaming onto Brian's skilled tongue.

I think I screamed.

When I came to my senses, I heard Brian moaning and sucking in my juices, lapping at me like I was his favorite dessert.

I was too sensitive, and I tried to roll away, but he smacked my ass again.

"Naughty, Bailey. I think it's high time you sucked my cock."

Oh, yes. Yes. I desperately wanted to taste that fat cock of his and give him a small percentage of the pleasure he'd just given me. I tried to roll off him, but he held me fast.

"Sixty-nine me, slut. I'm not done with this pussy just yet."

I made a strangled noise. More? I... I didn't know if I could do it.

"Brian..."

"You're mine right now, slut, and you'll do exactly what I say, or there will be consequences. Don't make me beat that round ass of yours even harder."

His hand came down again for good measure, stinging the spot he'd already hit. I bit my lip against the pain, then groaned as it mingled with my fading orgasm.

"Flip around and suck my dick, Bailey."

I did as he demanded, twisting so my pussy was over his face again, and I was leaning over his rock hard cock, glistening now with a bead of pre-cum. I lapped it up eagerly, savoring the salty taste of him, mingling with the musky smell of his balls. *Delicious.*

I slid my mouth over the fat head, suckling hard on the tip as Brian licked my too-sensitive folds. He groaned, and the vibration against my clit made me shriek. He slapped my ass harder.

"Hold still!"

"It's too much, Brian!"

I licked the length of his cock in protest, then shoved the whole thing in my mouth, relaxing until I felt it bump the back of my throat. I heard a growl before my ass was smacked again and again, so hard that I almost choked on his dick.

"You'll come again, you little bitch. You'll come all over my face, and you'll like it!"

God-damn. Brian was one hot motherfucker. All I could do was let him take control of my body and trust that he knew what he was doing. Hopefully he didn't kill me with all this pussy licking.

He continued his sensual assault on my folds, licking me up and down, then doing that crazy swirl of his until I couldn't stand any more. But, just as I was writhing on his face, I felt it building again—that sweet torture, spiraling up inside my belly.

I deep-throated his cock, running my tongue over the bottom ridge expertly as I let it tap my throat over and over. I wanted him to explode inside my mouth—wanted to taste his cum filling my throat and coating my tongue. I wanted to make him cum harder than he'd ever come in his life.

I wasn't one to be one-upped in the sack.

His balls tightened, and I cupped them, massaging them as I sucked him hard, tonguing him over and over as he mimicked my motions on my pussy. My thighs were trembling again, but I wanted him to be first. I hoovered his dick like I was siphoning gas, and I felt him gasp into my dripping cunt.

Oh, dammit, he was doing it again, the bastard! I tried to hold back, but his tongue swirled like gale force winds, and I tumbled over the edge into a pulsing, thigh clenching, screaming orgasm. I yelled around his cock.

His fingers dipped into my pussy, and I clenched hard around him as he finger fucked me, pumping first two, then three into me, making me buck back against him. Fuck me, but Brian was absolutely amazing at this.

I added a hand to his cock, twisting as I sucked the tip. A hand came down on my ass again, and I yelped.

"I want to come in that tight pussy of yours, Bailey. Give me that little cunt."

I released his cock with a wet *pop*, and rolled to the side.

"Ohhh, yes. I need it, Brian. Please! Fuck me."

I couldn't believe I was begging for it like this.

I felt like I'd been hit by a sexual freight train. I couldn't possibly come again. Everything was so sensitive it was almost painful. But I needed to know what it was like to have that thick cock stretching me before this night was through. And dammit, I needed to make this boy come. He'd more than earned it. I couldn't believe he hadn't blown yet. *Unbelievable.*

He got up and pulled me over to the edge of the bed, so I was on my back with my ass hanging over the edge. I felt like I was going to fall, but he nodded at me, as if saying "You can trust me." I nodded back, suddenly feeling shy. I was so exposed like this, completely trusting him not to drop me.

He pressed my thighs back, so my knees bumped my shoulders, then held me with one hand, and guided that monster cock of his to my entrance with the other. It was still wet with my saliva, but he rubbed it up and down my slit, lubricating the head with my arousal.

"Yes! Please..." I needed him. I couldn't stand it if he tortured me like this for much longer. I *had* to feel that cock in me.

He pressed into me, sliding just the head in and stopping, letting me adjust. I gasped. It was on the borderline between painful and delicious, filling me up in a way I'd never felt before. He wasn't the longest I'd had, but he was certainly the thickest. He reached between us and thumbed my clit, making me clench around him involuntarily. He grinned, then jammed the rest of his length into me in one sure stroke.

I cried out as he filled me completely. My mind was buzzing with sensation, filled to the brim with his magnificent dick. I writhed beneath him as he touched my clit, sending shocks through my pussy.

"No! Too mu-"

He slapped my tit, and I screeched.

"You're mine, Bailey, and I'll do what I want with this tight little body of yours!"

He slapped my other breast, making a red mark spring up, and my nipples tighten painfully with arousal.

"You're going to come again for me, whether you like it or not, slut!"

"No!"

Another slap, another sting on my tender flesh. "Fuck!"

He pumped in and out of me, slowly at first, then faster, driving his dick all the way to my cervix, then pulling back.

All the while, he brushed my clit slowly with his thumb. I wanted to slap his hand away, but the overwhelming stimulation was making me pant for breath.

I reached below my legs and stroked his balls, feeling them tighten in my grip. He pressed my legs back even further and changed the angle of his thrusts. I gasped as the tip of his cock slammed into my g-spot, making my pussy clench around him. I let my head fall back, surrendering to this boy—this man. He was seriously going to do it. He was going to take me there again.

He drove into me over and over again, hitting me hard in just the right spot, making me whine and gasp and mewl as he took me to a place I'd never imagined I'd reach. The tension build, but it was different this time. Deeper. Hotter. I wanted to flip him over and ride him—let him know *I* was in control, but I knew it was a lie. I was his to do with as he pleased. And the real surprise? I was loving every minute of it.

It came up on me fast, seizing me in its grip like a hand around my throat. I thrashed as I came, but he held me still, pinned beneath his grip as he pumped into me again and again, mercilessly thumbing my clit as I exploded around him.

I scratched his abs, wanting to pull him close, but he held my hips, driving into me like a piston. I yelled mindlessly, breaking apart beneath him. Finally, I heard him grunt, and yell my name.

"Bailey! Fuck. Yes!"

His cum splashed into my body, filling me with satisfaction, piercing through my fuzzy mind, as I still spasmed helplessly around him. He collapsed on top of me, holding me close, nuzzling in my hair. I wanted to wrap my legs around him, keep him there, but I was too exhausted.

We lay there for a long while, him kissing my face and neck, and me wrapping my hands in that black hair of his and trying to catch my breath. When I finally sat up, I didn't know what to say.

"Thank you," I whispered, then blushed and turned away.

He touched my chin, and looked deep into my eyes. "You were the best I've ever had, Bailey."

Tears sprang to my eyes, but I hastily brushed them away.

"You, too."

***

Later, when I stumbled back down the hall, bow-legged, in a pair of borrowed briefs and my tank top, I smiled in the darkness. I rubbed the sore spots on my breasts and ass, loving the sweet sting when I touched them.

Brian...

I pushed open the door of Amber's room to see the girls still sprawled out, dead to the world. I guess they hadn't heard my screams after all. Good.

I lay down next to Amber, feeling dirty about the fact that her brother's cum was still trickling from my pussy into his borrowed underwear, but also savoring the naughty feeling of getting away with something so major.

Savannah rolled over and grinned sleepily. "You nasty slut," she mumbled, then went back to sleep.

I snorted with laughter, then covered my mouth, not wanting to wake Amber.

She had no idea.

ABOUT THE AUTHOR

Delilah Fawkes is the bestselling erotic romance author of "The Billionaire's Beck and Call" series, selling more than 150,000 e-books in 2012.

She's known for sizzling romances with red hot alpha males you'll fall in love with and strong women who make them swoon.

If you like your romance gripping, fast-paced, and dripping with sinful love scenes, you've got to check out what Delilah has to offer.

Thank you again for reading—she couldn't do it without you!

Made in the USA
Lexington, KY
29 March 2013